THE GOLD
OF
BLACK MOUNTAIN

THE GOLD
OF BLACK
MOUNTAIN

•

Kent Conwell

AVALON BOOKS
NEW YORK

PRINTED IN THE UNITED STATES OF AMERICA
ON ACID-FREE PAPER
BY HADDON CRAFTSMEN, BLOOMSBURG, PENNSYLVANIA

To my family, Amy, Susan, and Gayle,
who understand the hours I spend at my desk.
Thanks for all your support and patience.

Chapter One

As a youngster up in the Redlands of east Texas, I remember that local folklore claimed that death, marriages, and trouble came in threes. When I hit twenty-seven, I learned that wasn't true—at least about trouble.

For me, it came in two's—two nuns, two little girls, and two Comancheros. Now that I think about it, that's three sets of twos. Who knows, maybe the old stories were right. But right or wrong, because of that odd assortment of folks, my life was never the same. I learned from them that the only difference between a rut and a grave is the depth.

One thing is for certain: If I had been in a rut, those females took me out of it.

The Civil War left Texas penniless. From Steve Austin's original three hundred to the newest settler, every Texan was as poor as Job's turkey. The only greenbacks in the state came with the carpetbaggers who swooped in like greedy buzzards. They bought businesses, plantations, and ranches at prices so low they were sinful.

Personally, I didn't call it buying. I called it stealing. Of course, I was paddling in the same canoe with all the other Texans. If a ten-course meal cost a dollar, I'd have been hard put to scrape up enough wampum for a spoonful of black-eyed peas.

As a result of the money shortage, cowpokes started hunting the south Texas brush for wild cattle—long-legged Mexican longhorns, critters ornerier than a stepped-on rattlesnake, meaner than scorpions, and always looking for the chance to stomp a body into a wet spot in the sand.

No matter the danger, brush popping became a popular business. Popular, deadly, but profitable. More than one hungry Texan spent a few months dragging wild cattle out of the chaparral to build a herd, then moving it north to the railhead, picking up a return of several thousand dollars. On the other hand, twice the number of Texas boys ended up nothing but grease smears on the desolate Texas prairie.

Ed McKeever and me decided if others could make a dollar from wild beeves, we could too. While we didn't have the funds to undertake a twelve-hundred-mile cattle drive, we decided to round up a couple hundred head and sell them to passing herds for a dollar or so each. And the two of us together should be enough to frighten away any skulking Indians.

For our first effort, we sold seventy-three head to Joe Barstow out of Jim Wells County; the second, a hundred twenty to Bob Trout Pringle, who was headed for Abilene.

It was in the middle of our third roundup that the brindle longhorn and I butted heads.

We had eighteen or nineteen of the wild critters corralled in a bend on Mission River well above Refugio when I spotted a mama longhorn with her calf. As soon as she laid eyes on me, she shot into the thick chaparral growing on a long ridge, her calf right on her heels. I jumped in behind them, laying out my loop.

Before I could get close, she dropped down the ridge into a forest of pecan and ash lining a narrow creek. I kept up the chase.

Staying on the heels of that long-legged bovine was like chasing a chicken. Once or twice, I almost lost the saddle when my mustang cut to stay with her. With a belligerent bawl, she shot up another ridge into a dense tangle of mesquite and scrub oak.

I laid out my loop again. The brush was so thick I had to hoolihan it out, a trick of tossing an underhanded loop that swept up from the ground to settle over the horns.

Well, it settled on that critter's horns, sure enough, and she started skywalking, shooting abruptly to her right. She moved so fast that before I could jerk the mustang around, the longhorn hit the end of the lariat.

The mustang grunted, and the cinch popped. My head snapped, and I flew through the air, still in the saddle.

Things sort of happened in slow motion then. I was still sitting upright in my saddle when I hit the ground. The next second, my bay mustang was twenty yards away, zigzagging through the thick mesquite, mane and tail whipping in the breeze, reins popping off the ground, and puffs of fine white dust billowing up from his feet.

I shook my head and shot a glance over my shoulder

just in time to see that two-thousand-pound longhorn lower her head and lunge at me. Sunlight glittered on the tips of her six-foot horns. I threw myself forward over the saddle horn just before she hooked. Lucky for me, she caught the saddle. Unlucky for me, I stayed in the saddle, spinning through the air with it. Just before everything went black, I remember hoping I didn't land in any of the patches of prickly pear with their inch-long spines.

When I opened my eyes, stars filled the night. I blinked once or twice, and the stars began spinning. The next time I awakened, the sun was directly overhead. I closed my eyes and breathed deeply. As life returned to my lanky frame, so did the pain.

My head pounded, my back ached, and my arm throbbed. I felt the tickle of the sweat as it rolled down the side of my head into my ears, beaded on my jaw, and dripped on my neck. Behind my closed lids, the sun was a red ball rolling around in my head.

A searing pain exploded in my skull. Clenching my teeth, I grabbed at my arm. One bone scraped another.

With a moan, I rolled over on my side and opened my eyes.

My heart jumped into my throat.

In the shade of a patch of prickly pear, just beyond arm's reach, lay coiled a diamondback rattlesnake, its spade-shaped head swaying back and forth. At such a short distance, I could clearly see its yellow eyes fixed on me, even the vertical black pupils. A black tongue flickered, testing the air.

I caught my breath, forgetting the pain in my arm.

For hour-long seconds, we stared at each other. From experience, I knew one of two things would take place. Either he would grow curious and explore the object on the ground before him, or he would decide to go his own way.

I didn't want to wait for him to decide.

Taking a deep breath, I held my broken forearm against my stomach and abruptly rolled away from the rattler. Something snagged my leather vest, and with a yelp, I leaped to my feet and fumbled for my six-gun with my good hand, ignoring the excruciating pain in my other arm.

By the time I turned around, the rattler was disappearing into the tanglehead and sandburr grass beyond the clump of prickly pear. I glanced at the ground at my feet and spotted a small mesquite stub. With a weak grin, I realized that's what had snagged my vest.

Gingerly, I slid my fractured arm into my shirt for a temporary sling while I unsheathed my knife and hacked four short limbs for splints. I tore my kerchief into strands and fastened them to the rough and crooked splints.

Wedging my hand into the fork of a mesquite, I took a deep breath and leaned back, feeling the bones scrape back into place. I groaned at the intense pain, which knocked me to my knees. I fought the wave of dizziness sweeping over me. Sucking in oxygen to lessen the pain, I leaned my head against the trunk of the mesquite.

After a few moments, I staggered to my feet and managed to tie the splints in place, immobilizing the forearm. I looped a sling over my neck and gently placed my arm in it.

With a groan, I sagged to my knees and leaned back against the trunk of the mesquite, my sweat-soaked clothes clinging to my body.

I passed out.

*   *   *

The insistent pain in my arm awakened me. Overhead, the stars glittered. A light breeze twisted through the thick chaparral, cooling my forehead. My arm throbbed, and it was hot to the touch, but the flesh wasn't broken.

At least, I had water. I crawled to my saddle and gratefully gulped half a dozen swallows of warm water. A cold beer never tasted so good.

I lay back on the saddle and closed my eyes. Then I remembered the rattler. Nighttime was hunting time for him, and a hundred others like him. Slowly rising, I peered into the darkness around me. The starlight illumined the oak and mesquite ridge with a bluish light.

More than once, I'd seen a rattler snatch a bird off the middle rail of a corral. I climbed a mesquite and settled into a high fork. I was in for a long night and little sleep, but at least I was beyond the reach of any prowling rattlesnake.

Chapter Two

I awakened before dawn, dripping with sweat. Every muscle in my body screamed when I tried to move from my cramped position. Clenching my teeth, I managed to roll off the mesquite limb. My boot caught in the fork, throwing me off balance. Without thinking, I threw out my broken arm to catch myself.

The searing pain, dulled by sleep, exploded in my head. I hit the ground and grabbed my arm to my chest, cursing through clenched teeth. I lay on my back, gasping in great gulps of air. Slowly, the pain subsided to a dull throbbing.

To the east, the sky grew lighter, pushing the darkness back. Shaking from the pain, I crawled to my saddle and drank some water. The cool liquid soothed my parched throat and lips. I sat motionless, staring at the faint gray of false dawn. For the first time since the longhorn ripped the saddle from my mustang, I tried to focus my thoughts.

As best I could recollect through the cobwebs in my

head, I'd been out here two nights. Where was my partner, Ed McKeever? If my mustang had gone back to camp—and there was no reason to think otherwise—then McKeever had to know something was wrong.

I remained silent, staring at the sky growing lighter by the minute. "One thing's certain, old hoss," I mumbled to myself. "Chances are, no one's going to haul your worthless carcass out of here except you."

Forcing a wry chuckle, I staggered to my feet. No one in my life had hauled my worthless carcass anywhere. Since I was twelve, everything I had done, I had to do it myself, even if it wasn't much. I slung the canteen around my neck and my saddlebags over my good arm.

Glancing around at my surroundings, I mumbled. "Well, Jack Edward Burnett, which way is which?"

I swayed on my feet. I was weak as pond water. I dug out some jerky from my saddlebags and worried off a chunk. Jerky isn't steak, and it isn't tender, but it did provide me the energy and strength I needed to start my journey. Slowly, I headed northwest. If I remembered right, our camp shouldn't be more than a mile or so. I still wondered about McKeever.

The morning sun rose, quickly drying the dew. The air was thick with moisture rising from the grass, a thick, suffocating wetness.

I staggered down a ridge. My feet tangled in some berry briars, and I stumbled to the ground. I lay motionless for several seconds, catching my breath before continuing.

I lost count of the number of times I lurched and fell, but the last time I fell was into the refreshing waters of the Mission River. I lay motionless for what seemed like hours, letting the cool water soothe my aching muscles and soak my throbbing arm.

While I lay on the riverbank, a tiny water snake swam past. Thanks to the jerky, I wasn't hungry enough for raw snake. Despite my throbbing arm, I chuckled. "But if you hang around here much longer, Jack, you'll get that hungry."

I sat up and splashed water on my face and in my hair. I stared at my reflection in the water, at the painfully thin face that was nothing more than skin over bone. My ma always swore I was skinny enough to poke through a keyhole, and now a couple days without solid grub had hollowed my eyes and sunk my cheeks even more.

A distant rumble of thunder stirred me.

Wearily, I pushed myself to my feet. River water had soaked my pants and leather *chaparreras*, so I had to cinch up both belts around my gaunt waist to keep them from falling. Painfully, I made my way upriver in the direction of our camp, at each step half-expecting to hear the bawling of cattle or the thud of hoof beats. Instead, the only sounds that broke the stifling silence were the angry chatter of bluejays and the sharp replies of the tiny sparrows.

I hit a familiar path and hurried my steps. The silence was uncomfortable. A tingling started in the back of my neck. I paused, searching the thick undergrowth of huckleberries and wild azalea beneath the oak and pecan trees growing along the river. Grimacing, I shifted my gunbelt until the holster rested on my left hip. Awkwardly, I flipped the leather thong off the hammer and slid my six-gun from the holster.

In the distance, a crow cawed. Behind me came an answering cry. Comanche? Possibly, though most of them had their hands full with Colonel McKenzie up in the Texas Panhandle.

Forcing the constant pain in my arm from my head, I dropped into a crouch and eased forward. Our camp was around the next curve in the trail. I paused behind a patch of prickly pear at the bend and eased to one knee, peering through the tangle of wild huckleberry and blackberry briars.

The camp was deserted.

"What the . . . ?" I frowned as I studied the camp. The fire was only a pile of ashes, and our lean-to had collapsed, but our warbags remained. Fifteen or twenty longhorns milled about at one end of the corral. I spotted my mustang and McKeever's bay. But something was out of kilter. Where was McKeever? Had something happened to him? I eased forward.

Through the canopy of leaves overhead, I spotted circling buzzards.

A curse formed on my lips, then abruptly, a cold chill sent shivers racing through my body. A man lay on the ground in the rear of the corral, just above the water's edge.

Instinctively, I pressed back into the briars and huckleberries, my gaze quartering the camp quickly. Nothing moved.

Cautiously, I crept toward the corral. Overhead, a mockingbird jabbered. I remained in the shade, avoiding the glare of the sun, which could blind me momentarily.

When I grew closer, I made out a leg and an arm extended. The man was spread-eagled. I shivered despite the heat. I knew the identity of the inert figure, but I refused to admit the truth to myself, as if not saying it could keep it from being so.

Staying in the dense understory vegetation, I slipped around the corral for a closer look. Each step reaffirmed my initial fear. The man lay bare-chested, arms and legs fastened to stakes. Glancing around, I dropped into a crouch behind a small hackberry, studying the figure. I stared at Ed McKeever.

I remained motionless for several minutes, searching the thick chaparral. Were those responsible still around?

As the heat rose from the packed ground in waves, it distorted the slow-moving waters of the river. Beads of sweat rolled down my spine.

Hearing or seeing nothing out of place, I slipped through the oak rails and instantly knelt, scanning the silent thicket around me. I glanced at McKeever.

No movement.

Keeping my eyes on the ominous chaparral beyond the corral, I crawled to McKeever, ignoring the nickering of our ponies or the one or two snorting longhorns. I jerked to a halt when I saw my partner. Fat, green flies darted in every direction. He had died in a horrible way. The faint odor of the first stages of putrefaction assailed my nostrils. I forced the rising gorge back down my throat.

The crack of a branch from deep in the forest beyond the corral froze me momentarily, then quickly I scrabbled back to the cover of the thicket and knelt beside a thick patch of briars.

I waited, my gaze searching the underbrush left to right, up and down. Flies buzzed in swirling formations above the piles of cow patties in the corral.

Another snap, and then came a rustling of leaves.

I thumbed back the hammer and raised my six-gun.

The rustling grew closer.

My breathing grew fast. I dragged my tongue over my dry lips and tightened my finger on the trigger.

A moment later, a deer stepped from the under-brush, paused, and, with its head held high, searched the corral and the open area surrounding it. I released my pent-up breath with a groan.

The deer shot sideways, vanishing instantly into the undergrowth.

I leaned forward against the hackberry and closed my eyes. The last surge of tension drained me of my strength. I remained unmoving, scarcely breathing, try-ing to rebuild my energy.

Another crackle of leaves followed by the crack of a branch sounded from deep in the ash and hickory forest beyond the corral.

Again I raised my six-gun. I needed meat, and al-though I could not carry an entire deer, I could slice off enough venison to get me to Goliad.

The cracking of branches and the rustling of leaves ceased. I eased behind the hackberry and laid the bar-rel of my revolver on a branch for a rest. I wasn't much of shot right-handed, and am almost useless with my left.

Abruptly, a Mexican wearing a wide sombrero rode out of the chaparral. He wore a bright red and yellow sash around his heavy belly. His face was scarred with smallpox. He reined up, a sneer twisting his thick lips. He scanned the corral and called out. "Manuel! Hey, hombre."

Hey, hombre? I crouched lower. He had a compadre about. But where?

He called out again. "Aqui. Come."

I heard water splashing behind me. I looked over my shoulder, but the vegetation was too thick to see the river. Moments later, a second Comanchero rode from the river into the corral.

Ignoring McKeever, they put their ponies in the corral and replaced the rails, after which they built up a fire and rustled grub from their warbags.

I considered pot-shotting them, but left-handed at twenty yards? My chances were worse than those of a chicken dropped into a roomful of foxes.

Silently, I eased into as comfortable a position as I could manage and waited. For what, I didn't know. An opportunity. An opening of some kind. A miracle.

The second Comanchero, the one called Manuel, removed a gourd from his saddle, popped a cork from the handle, and turned it up. He gulped noisily, wiped the back of his hand across his lips, and handed it to his partner.

Tequila or mescal, I guessed.

I waited, watching my miracle unfold.

To the west, dark clouds filled the sky.

Two hours later, after a meal of roasted venison and a full gourd of whiskey, they slept. The approaching storm clouds brought an early dusk.

My arm throbbed, the steady pain numbing it and pounding in my ears.

I peered through the growing darkness at McKeever. I tightened my finger on the trigger. One way or another, I was going to get some payback for him.

Thunder rumbled. Streaks of lightning flashed across the western sky.

The Comancheros appeared to be sleeping soundly, the combination of a full belly and overabundance of whiskey doing the trick. Before darkness completely settled in, I eased to my feet and took a step forward.

Slowly, I lined the barrel on the one of the sleeping Mexicans.

Abruptly, thunder exploded and lightning flashed. In the eerie silver-white light of the lightning, the Comanchero and I stared at each other. He jerked back just as I fired.

I missed. Frantically, I tried to thumb back the hammer, but my left thumb slipped. I cursed and leaped back into the underbrush, heading for the river. The briars scraped against my *chaparreras* and leather vest, like fingers grasping at my legs and chest.

Shots echoed behind me, drowning out the shouts of the angry Comancheros. A lead plum smacked into the trunk of a live oak half a dozen steps from me.

I stumbled onto the trail and bolted down it. Tearing through the underbrush, the Comancheros came storming after me, intent on sending me to heaven to look for a harp.

One second the dim light diffused over the forest, showing the path. The next second I couldn't make out the trail at my feet. Suddenly, my boots dropped from under me, and I tumbled head over heels into the cold waters of the Mission River.

The excited voices coming from the forest were garbled. They faded as I drifted downstream. I didn't know where I was going, but anywhere would be better than where I had been.

Chapter Three

I treaded water, squinting into the coal-black darkness surrounding me, biting my bottom lip to keep from crying out from the pain shooting up my arm.

Between peals of lightning, I heard splashing in the water upriver, then silence.

In the middle of the stream, the heavy current pulled at me. Coughing and sputtering, I fought to keep my head above water. Heavy boots, soaked duck trousers, leather *chaparreras*, and one arm don't lend themselves to staying afloat without a struggle. I unbuckled my chaps, sending them to the bottom, and then I battled toward the far shore.

A tangle of dead limbs swept down on me, gouging at my face. I threw my arm over them and allowed them to carry me downstream. The storm struck. A torrent of rain fell, obliterating everything beyond arm's length.

Lightning cracked and flashed, lighting the silver rain with an eerie glow. I lost track of how long I had drifted, but when I struck the lee shore of a bend, I lay in the mud without moving, content for the water to rush over me in its headlong journey downriver.

The storm intensified. I felt the water rising.

Somehow I clambered up the bank and collapsed at the base of an ancient live oak. I fell into an exhausted sleep, too weary to worry about what the next day would bring.

I'm not sure just what awakened me. Overhead, robins and sparrows sang from the treetops. Beyond the canopy of leaves, the sky was fresh-washed blue. I could even smell the heavy fragrance of blooming shrubs. Then I heard the noise again, a rattling of wood and jangling of metal. A wagon. Someone was approaching in a wagon.

Moments later, high-pitched voices floated through the silent forest, and to my surprise I made out the words of the old trail song, *Get Along Little Doggies*. I propped myself up on my good arm and shook my head, clearing the sleep. Were my ears playing tricks?

The next words assured me I'd heard correctly. Through the forest came the chorus of the song.

I didn't wait to hear the rest of the chorus. I lumbered to my feet and staggered through the underbrush, trying to shout, trying to warn the travelers of the Comancheros.

I crashed through the thick vegetation and stumbled onto a trail, a faint trace that appeared to lead from Refugio to Goliad, home of the Presidio La Bahia, near the San Antonio River, where Fannin and his men died.

I reeled on my feet, but I had to warn the wagon. I stumbled around the bend and jerked to a halt. Two nuns in those black dresses and two young girls were staring back at me.

I knew I looked downright scary. Water-soaked, dirty, unshaven. I held up my good hand. "I . . . I don't mean no harm." I pointed behind me. "Comancheros . . . up there. They . . ." A wave of unconsciousness threatened me. "They killed my partner. Don't . . ."

That was the last I remember until I awakened that night.

I lay in a tent of sorts, three-sided, in which a small fire flickered. The buckboard, draped with a tarp, sat on the fourth side.

The two girls and one nun slept. The other nun was kneeling beside the wagon, her head bowed in prayer.

"Wh . . . where are we?" My words were nothing more than a raw croak.

The praying nun quickly crossed herself, then looked at me and smiled. "You must be thirsty." She came to my side with a red clay mug of water and helped me sit up. I gulped so fast I choked myself. Gently, she patted my back. "Slow now. Slow. There's plenty more."

The sister glided around the campfire, returning moments later with a bowl of simmering stew. Humming softly, she fed me. The stew was rich and filling with tender chunks of meat and flavorsome vegetables.

When I awakened again, the sun was high overhead. My arm throbbed. Someone had freshly dressed it. I looked up. The young girls were staring at me.

The younger one, freckle-faced and pug-nosed, jumped to her feet and disappeared into the forest. The other, dark-haired and serious, poured me a cup of water. "Here," she said. "The sisters will be right back."

Seconds later, the two nuns returned, arms laden with roots and tubers from the forest, enough grub for a couple days if you prefer vegetables to meat. The older one dumped her load and knelt beside me, placing her hand on my forehead. She had a face like a baby. "You look stronger. How is the arm?"

The pain was still there, but not as intense. "Better, thanks. Lucky for me, it wasn't a bad break."

"Good. I am Sister Rossetta, and this . . ." She indicated the younger nun. "This is Sister Alicia." She hesitated, then added, "A novice."

Sister Alicia gave me a shy smile and quickly turned away.

Sister Rossetta laid her hand on the little brown-haired girl's shoulder. "This is Carmaline, and the little one with all the beautiful freckles is Mary Elizabeth. We're from Indianola."

I nodded. "Thanks" was all I could say.

Sister Rossetta arched an eyebrow. "And what do we call you, my son?"

I looked around the camp, searching the underbrush.

Her smile broadened. "We are safe. I moved us into the chaparral away from the trace. We've seen no sign of those you mentioned." She laid her hand on mine, and a strange feeling of security came over me. "Now, what do we call you?"

"Jack." I cleared my throat. "Jack Edward Burnett, Sister." I glanced at Sister Alicia, but she kept her eyes averted, intent on peeling the tubers and roots.

"Are you hungry, Mr. Burnett?"

My stomach growled like an angry cougar. I was

famished. "Yes, ma'am, I sure am." I sat up and Carmaline brought me a bowl of stew.

More times than I could remember, I'd gone without food, so I knew enough not to shovel it down my gullet like a hog, but instead to take it nice and slow. Between bites I asked, "You haven't seen any strangers, huh?"

Sister Rossetta shook her head. "No. You mentioned you saw some Comancheros. They are very bad people."

I swallowed another bite. "Yes, ma'am. They're back north of us a piece. Or they were. My partner and I had a small camp on the creek." I told her the whole story, skipping the gory details out of respect for their gender.

When I finished, Sister Rossetta's smile had dimmed. "They've not passed this way. Although we are well off the Goliad Trace, we would have heard them." She smiled brightly at the girls. "My two young fledglings here have the ears of a fox. Isn't that so, girls?"

The girls' eyes danced. They nodded. "Yes, Sister," Mary Elizabeth replied.

I studied the situation. "I reckon, then, they went north toward the San Antone River." I paused, remembering when I had first spotted the nuns and children. They were heading north, too. My words stuck in my throat, but I managed to cough them out. "The same direction you folks were heading, Sister."

Unperturbed, she nodded. "Yes. Goliad, then north to Gonzales."

"Gonzales? But that's at least a hundred miles, and over dangerous country. Dangerous for anyone, but especially two nuns and two children. . . ."

The four exchanged quick glances. Sister Alicia returned to her cooking, and the girls buried their heads in some soft-covered books.

Sister Rossetta noticed me staring at the girls. She explained. "Catechisms. Part of their lessons."

"Catechisms?"

"Yes. Questions and answers of our beliefs, part of their religious training."

The throbbing in my arm intensified. I tried to shift it around to ease the pain, but nothing relieved the constant pounding. I tried to ignore the throbbing, push it to the back of my mind. "What religion is that, Sister?"

She smiled warmly at me, the kind of smile that would make anyone feel good. "We are of the Sisters of the Holy Father St. Matthew. We came to the Texas coast to establish a hospital and school much like the one we did in Tucson."

"So what's in Gonzales?"

"Actually, Mr. Burnett, I am going beyond Gonzales. To the Colorado River beyond Austin."

I gaped. "Austin? Why, that's another fifty or sixty miles." I paused. "Same question then, Sister. What's in Austin?"

The smile on her face broadened with the innocence of a child. "Why, the gold to build our mission."

I stared at her a moment, stunned. Then I glanced at the two girls busy with their catechisms. My gaze shifted to Sister Alicia, who busied herself over the iron pot of stew. For the moment, I forgot about the pain in my arm. "G-gold?" I stared at her, wondering from the twinkle in her eye if she was joshing me. "You're not serious, are you, Sister?"

"Why, yes." A puzzled expression replaced the

smile on her cherubic face. "Is there something wrong?"

I had the feeling I was in the middle of a dream. Here were two nuns and two girls in a buckboard, trekking through the wilds of south Texas in search of gold. An impossible journey. They might as well try walking through the Gates of Hades barefoot.

The trip didn't make sense. No one with reasonable intelligence would undertake such a task unless they were outfitted with plenty of grub, weapons, and pack horses. I hesitated. I didn't want to offend her, but whether she knew it or not their lives were at serious risk. The fact that they were of a religious order meant nothing to roaming Comanches or vicious Comancheros.

I cleared my throat. "Look, Sister, I'm much obliged to you for the help. Even if you folks hadn't given me a hand, I couldn't stand by and see you walking directly into more trouble than you ever imagined was on God's green earth."

"Holy Father St. Matthew will look after us, Mr. Burnett."

Her naïve belief in that St. Matthew hombre exasperated me. I'd never heard of St. Matthew. I wasn't sure who he was, but I knew he couldn't pick up a .44 caliber Remington New Model Army revolver and fight off a passel of Comancheros.

"I don't know, Sister. I'm not much of a religious hombre, but I reckon this St. Matthew jasper will help those who help themselves. Trust in the Lord, but don't stop fighting. At least that's what my mother always taught me about the good Lord. He'll help those who help themselves. And that doesn't include walking into the middle of trouble without any way to take care of yourself.''

"Trust in Him, Mr. Burnett. Trust in Him.'' She folded her hands into the sleeves of her habit. "He will look after us, Mr. Burnett. He has so far.''

The girls continued reading, and Sister Alicia stirred the simmering pot over the fire. Sister Rossetta's blind confidence in His protection was frustrating and, at the same time, almost admirable. She had no idea of the dangers they faced. "Sometimes, Sister, this St. Matthew might need some help. You ever think about that?''

Her smile grew wider. "Oh yes.''

Finally, a chip in her convictions. Maybe she was beginning to realize that her Holy Father couldn't do it all himself. Naturally, I was wrong. The story of my life.

"Oh yes, we knew we could never complete the journey on our own, Mr. Burnett. So we prayed, and St. Matthew answered our prayers.''

Sister Alicia and the girls looked up at me. They nodded as one.

For some strange reason, I had the feeling that I wasn't going to like Sister Rossetta's next remark. "After all, Mr. Burnett,'' she said calmly, "why do you think he sent you to us?''

I shook my head, uncertain I had heard her right. "Huh?''

Sister Alicia and the girls were smiling at me now. Sister Rossetta nodded. "St. Matthew sent you to us. You are our helping hand.''

Chapter Four

A cool breeze rippled the flames of the small fire. A mouth-watering aroma drifted from the stew Sister Alicia was stirring. Behind Sister Rossetta, a robin landed on a branch and whistled merrily. A second joined in.

All was right with the world. Except for me. I stammered for words.

"What exactly do you mean, I'm your helping hand?"

She smiled. It was the smile of contentment, of a woman who had everything she wanted and needed. "Just what I said, Mr. Burnett. You see, before you came into our lives, we said twenty novenas to St. Matthew for a sign that we were doing as he wished. We knew our journey would be difficult, and that we did indeed need assistance. We had sought help along the way, but none would come to our aid. Then you came along. St. Matthew sent you to us. You are our sign, and our helping hand."

I blinked not once but several times. She was right that I couldn't leave them by themselves, but there was no way I was going to tromp about the state searching for gold with them. I had other plans, namely, tracking down the Comancheros who killed my partner and stole our stock.

"Look, Sister, I appreciate your help, and I do plan on sticking with you to Goliad. But then I've got plans of my own, and digging for gold isn't one of them."

She surprised me again. I'd expected the smile on her face to turn into a frown. It just grew wider, and the twinkle in her eyes glittered a little more. "Oh no, Mr. Burnett. Believe me, you're the one. You'll be with us until we find the gold."

Sister Alicia gave me a big smile and returned to her work. Carmaline and Mary Elizabeth giggled at each other before going back to their catechisms.

I don't like arguing. Never have. Besides, this woman was too stubborn for her own good. Let her think what she wanted. I'd stay with them to Goliad, then they were on their own. "Well, Sister, I think your St. Matthew made a mistake this time, but I'm not going to argue with you."

That evening, I scouted ahead just in case the Comancheros were still around. The camp was deserted. All our gear had been stolen. Even McKeever's body was missing. I studied the river for a few minutes, wondering.

I traipsed downstream along the shore on the outside chance I might find McKeever for a Christian burial. There was no sign of him. I stared at the moving waters. "So long, partner," I muttered, reluctantly turning back into the forest toward camp.

* * *

We pulled out before sunrise the next morning. Sister Rossetta handled the team, a pink-eyed white and a snaky bay, two churn-headed animals as mismatched as I was with the nuns. I rode on the seat with her, my good hand resting on the butt of my six-gun.

The country around us was lush, green, and vast. If I hadn't spent all my time searching the trees and surrounding chaparral for Comancheros, I would have reveled at the majestic hickories, towering pecans, and elms lining the river. Off to our right, mesquite and chaparral grew in almost impenetrable thickets. Along the river, under the shade of the hardwoods, the breeze was cool, carrying with it the sharp scent of the tall junipers.

Along the trace where the sun managed to break through, the bluestem and Indiangrass grew so thick and tender that a jasper could have raised a six-month calf in two months. Rabbits feeding on the succulent grass were thicker than warts on a bullfrog. For the most part, they simply ignored us, scooting a few feet out of our way as we passed.

Had the weather been cold, we could have enjoyed rabbit broiled, baked, roasted, or fricasseed. But during the warm months, rabbit fever was too much of a risk.

We reached Mission Nuestra Señora del Rosario just before dusk of the second day. Franciscan monks invited us to spend the night. I declined. "Goliad's only a few miles farther, Sister Rossetta. If I can borrow one of the horses, I'll ride in and take care of some business. I'll return the pony in the morning." She agreed, and I swung on the white. Sitting on the horse's back was like straddling a rail fence.

Carmaline spoke up, her voice thin and frail. "Be careful, Mr. Burnett."

I looked at her solemn face and large brown eyes. "Thanks, child."

A couple miles outside of Goliad, I reached the Presidio La Bahia, the fort by the bay. I reined up and stared at the silent stone structure, at the chapel tower looming over the dark walls, the chapel where the Texans were held prisoners. I remembered my pa and grandpa around the fireplace at night, talking in hushed tones of the gruesome deeds that Santa Anna had executed.

My most riveting memory was of the virulent anger with which my grandpa cursed the Mexican leader for murdering the Texans here at La Bahia and leaving their bodies to rot.

The day was Palm Sunday. No Texan could forget that. And no Texan could forget the bodies lying unburied until June 3, when General Thomas Rusk and his army gathered the pitiful remains and buried them.

With a click of my tongue, I sent the horse toward Goliad, a flickering of dim lights in the distance. I tried to put the animal in a gait that wouldn't jar my arm, but the only stride that didn't send spasms of pain up my arm was a walk, and that took too long. I clenched my teeth and kicked him into a gentle lope.

Goliad was a lazy little village, its adobe and jacale buildings standing ramshackle around the town square. On the north side of the square stood the hanging tree, an ancient live oak. For thirty years, the rugged tree's canopy of leaves had served as a courthouse and its limbs a convenient means to carry out the execution of the sentence.

I pulled up at the saloon, an old adobe on the corner across from the town square. Several more cow horses were tied at the rail. A weathered sign hung above the door with equally weathered letters:

THE GALLANT TEXAN.

Arching an eyebrow, I ambled inside and headed for the bar. The undercurrent of murmuring ceased. I felt eyes on my back, but that was natural. Anytime a stranger showed up, especially at this time of night, most hombres who frequented the saloon were a bit leery.

The canvas ceiling sagged so much from water and dirt, I had to duck as I passed. At the bar, I ordered a whiskey. While I waited, I glanced at myself in the chipped mirror behind the collection of whiskey bottles. I looked like I'd be spit out and stomped on.

"Here you be, mister." The barkeep slid the drink down the bar. He was a short man with a crooked nose.

I fumbled in a vest pocket for a coin and slid a half eagle to him. "Thanks. Leave the bottle." I planned on a few drinks to numb the throbbing in my arm.

"Many strangers come through?"

Every eye in the room focused on me. Tension in the dimly lit room grew heavy.

He shrugged. "Some."

"I'm looking for a couple Mexicans. Comancheros. They hit our camp back south of here. Killed my partner and ran off with our stock." I drained my glass and poured another.

The tension lightened. A few murmurs broke out

behind me. The bartender shook his head and ran a slender finger over the bridge of his nose.

"Nope. Ain't seen no Mexican roundabouts other than them what lives around here. Them we got here are right good folks. Them Comanchero jugheads you're looking for ain't likely to show up around here."

I grimaced. I hadn't expected much luck, but you never know until you ask. "Yeah, I figured as much."

A voice behind me spoke up. "Old Jim Turner lives down on the south road to Refugio. He mighta seen something."

I downed my drink, poured another, and turned to face the speaker. "How do I find this Turner?"

"Ain't hard." He hooked a thumb to his left. "Take the road south to the first fork. Turn east half a mile. Old Jim's place is a clear patch cut out of the mesquite and scrub. Can't miss it."

"Much obliged, stranger." I downed my whiskey and nodded to the half-empty bottle on the bar. "How much for the rest?"

The bartender pointed to the half eagle. "This'll cover it."

"Thanks. Got a sack?"

He tossed me a soiled feed sack. "Been wiping the bar with it."

"It'll do." I dropped the bottle in the sack and knotted the neck around my belt.

Outside I swung onto the white and headed out of town. By now, I had a warm glow in my belly and the throbbing in my arm had dulled. And I had my own medicine.

* * *

A dim yellow light glimmered through the cracks in Jim Turner's jacale shack. I pulled in at his front door and dropped the knotted reins on the white's neck. "Jim Turner, you inside?" I remained astride the pony, holding my good hand over my head.

A voice crackled from the darkness to my right. "Get the other hand up, mister."

With a chuckle, I replied, "Like to, but it's busted. Got it in a sling."

I heard the pad of moving feet. When the voice spoke again, it had moved directly behind me so that if I were holding a gun, I'd have to twist halfway around in the saddle to take a shot. "Who you be, mister?"

"Jack Burnett. If you're Jim Turner, the old boys in town at the saloon sent me out here to you. If you're not Jim Turner, I sure ain't looking for trouble."

He snorted. "They did, did they?"

"Yep. I'm looking for a couple Comancheros."

His old voice was brittle with distrust. "Partners of yours?"

"Not quite. They killed my partner and stole our animals. I'm after them."

A moment of silence. The voice moved again. "What'd they look like?"

"Typical Mexican. Sombreros. One wore a bright red and yellow sash. Big belly."

More silence. Then from another spot in the darkness. "Seen a couple yesterday back east. Pushing beeves and ponies north. Likely up to Cuero where they'd sell'm to one of the drives heading up the Chisholm."

"One was fat. The one with the bright-colored sash. His face was scarred."

"Reckon that was them what I seen." Jim Turner grew silent.

There was nothing more to say. "Obliged, Mr. Turner. I'll ride out now."

He said nothing. Lowering my hand, I took the reins and turned the white back toward Goliad.

The small village was dark when I rode back in. I pulled into a livery. A barn lantern glowed dimly over a handful of ponies standing silently in the stalls. I found an empty one for the white, gave him some grain and hay, dropped a dollar in the can nailed just below the barn lantern, and then found myself a spot in the hay.

I took another large dose of medicine before I dropped off to sleep.

Next morning before sunrise, I haggled with the hostler over a willow-tailed chestnut with a sway belly and a well-worn saddle, a centerfire rig with no fenders, only the stirrup leathers. That dried-up old livery man was tighter than a corset on a saloon girl. The one concession I managed was a patched poncho and a fairly new saddle blanket, so the worn saddle forks wouldn't rub the bay raw. I handed over thirty dollars and stuck my last three greenbacks deep in my pocket.

During the ride back to the mission, I decided that since I was heading in the same direction as the sisters, we might as well travel together. Once we reached Cuero, they'd have to be on their own.

An hour later, I reached the Mission Nuestra Señora del Rosario. The sisters and the children were waiting at the buckboard, their gear stowed, the bay in harness.

I tied the chestnut to a wheel. While I harnessed the white to the bay, I told Sister Rossetta that I intended to ride on up to Cuero with them.

The girls clapped. Sister Alicia ducked her head.

Sister Rossetta's smile was so wide, I thought it would split that baby face of hers. She nodded to Sister Alicia and the girls, then turned back to me. "I knew you would, Mr. Burnett. The Holy Father St. Matthew sent you to us."

For a moment, I stared at her. That St. Matthew jasper hadn't sent me nowhere. I was after the Comancheros, and it just so happened they were forking their ponies in the same direction. I gestured to the buckboard. "Whatever you say, Sister. Right now, we're ready to head out." By now, I'd figured out she had that St. Matthew idea fixed in her head tighter than a double granny knot. No sense in arguing. Might as well talk to a stump.

Without any trouble, Cuero was a good two- or three-day ride to the north. I rode ahead of the buckboard, just in case there was trouble.

Summer in Texas is hot, even along the watercourses, but summer out in the south Texas chaparral is akin to being in one of those fancy steambaths without a door. The thickets of mesquite, spiny hackberry, blue sage, all twisted up by briars, stopped the breeze. By the time it wound its way through the warren of underbrush, the few exhausted tendrils of air were scorching.

The trail cut straight through the chaparral country. The nearest water was fifteen miles north. Slowly, we trudged along the trace. Despite the stifling heat and the suffocating dust billowing up from our feet, the sisters and the girls sang ditties, church hymns, and traveling songs. Sweat rolled down my spine. All I could do was shake my head at their energy and keep riding.

Around one o'clock we stopped in a patch of thin shade for grub and a couple hours' rest. Unless a jasper's got a posse on his tail, he's smart to stay out of the Texas sun from one to about three or so.

So we laid up in the shade, downed a bite of grub, and I snoozed a bit. The girls wandered around the camp, pointing out birds, giggling over butterflies, and shaking the heads off dandelions.

Sister Rossetta prayed a long time. I didn't notice Sister Alicia praying, but I'm certain she did. Seems like nuns always were praying, at least for the most part.

We moved out around four o'clock, planning on getting another three hours or so of travel. Less than half an hour up the trace, the thin breeze seemed to shift from the southerly currents at our backs. I ignored it, figuring it had somehow gotten itself twisted up in all the underbrush.

I glanced at the blue sky overhead. Clear as spring water.

The trace curved around the small ridges, staying on level ground. I glanced over my shoulder at the buckboard. I had to hand it to Sister Rossetta. She was a fair hand with the horses.

We were gradually moving farther onto the plains. A gust of wind struck my face. I looked up. A thin cloud drifted south through a brittle blue sky.

I reined up and studied the sky over my head. Engulfed by the thick chaparral, I couldn't see too much. With a click of my tongue, I sent the chestnut up a ridge where I could get a better look.

Back to the north and northeast, wispy clouds lay on the horizon. Even as I watched, they appeared to rise above the distant treetops. Back east, more clouds filled the sky, moving south.

I muttered a curse. We were in for some wet weather. Just how wet, I couldn't tell—not yet anyway. But unless I was sorely mistaken, a storm from off the Gulf of Mexico had blown in back south of us and was headed northwest across the state.

Chapter Five

I'm usually not wrong about storms and cattle. I wasn't this time either. Before dark, a few sprays of light rain blew in on us from the northeast. We made an early camp in a thick patch of mesquite and scrub oak and rigged the tarps for a snug shelter against the approaching weather.

Using my bad arm sparingly, I hobbled the animals and tied them in a thick copse of chaparral. The thorny brush made an ideal fence. The animals would get wet, but the undergrowth would break the wind.

By the time I returned to our three-sided shelter, Sister Alicia had a pot of soup on the fire. The top of the tent sagged from the rain. I hacked down a slender oak and, with the help of Carmaline, placed it in the middle of the roof and forced the top up, letting the rainwater run down the sides and spill to the ground.

"Good job," I said to her when we finished.

She beamed. Mary Elizabeth spoke up. "I want to help, too."

Sister Rossetta's eyes twinkled, and she gave me a smile.

"Next time, girl," I said. "Next time."

A pout clouded her face. "My name is Mary Elizabeth, Mr. Burnett. Not girl."

My cheeks burned. I gave Sister Alicia a sheepish grin. "Sorry, Mary Elizabeth. I'll remember."

"Now, girls, leave Mr. Burnett along. Come eat." Sister Rossetta shooed the youngsters back to their side of the tent.

Sister Alicia handed me a bowl of steaming soup. Our fingers touched, and it seemed like a tiny piece of lightning jumped between our fingertips.

She turned away abruptly.

With a bowl of hot soup in my stomach and a dry bed on which to sleep, I was content as an old he coon rolled up in a hollow trunk. I finished the soup with a smack. "Tasty, Sister Alicia, real tasty."

She smiled at me, and I noticed the firelight flicker in her eyes. She was a right pretty young woman, and I was sort of puzzled as to why someone so fine looking would want to be a nun. Yet I didn't know why I should be. Maybe it was because she didn't look like a nun—not the way Sister Rossetta did.

Carmaline and Mary Elizabeth stared at me. When they saw me staring back, they looked away quickly.

"How's your arm, Mr. Burnett?" Sister Rossetta smiled. "We might need to put a dry dressing on it."

I shook my head. "It's okay, Sister. This one'll dry out. Besides, it's going to get wet again tonight."

She frowned. "You mean you're going out in this weather?"

"The smart thing to do, Sister. Have to check the animals, both the four-legged and two-legged."

"Oh." She arched an eyebrow. "You think the Comancheros might be nearby?"

"Can't say." I threw on my poncho. "But I sure don't want to take a chance. If they're around, most likely the weather is bad enough to keep them holed up." I rose and pulled my hat down about my ears. "I'll go take a look around."

One step outside our shelter, and I knew no one would be out tonight. With the rain, I couldn't see more than an arm's length in front of me. That meant no one else could either.

Lowering my head into the storm, I felt my way to the animals. They had turned their tails to the storm. By feel, I checked their ropes. Still snug. Blindly, I worked my way back to the tent. Even at such a short distance, I couldn't make out any light. We were safe, at least for tonight.

I draped the wet poncho over the open side of the shelter to break some of the damp that swirled around the corners. Removing my hat, I squatted by the fire, gratefully taking a mug of coffee from Sister Alicia. The rain beat against the taut canvas. I shivered and sipped the strong liquid. A dollop of whiskey would have sure taste mighty good then and there. I glanced at my saddlebags where I'd stashed my bottle.

Reluctantly, I decided to pass it up. Given my present company, I doubted if I would have felt comfortable sipping whiskey.

"All is well, Mr. Burnett?" Sister Rossetta looked at me, a mischievous grin on her face.

"Yes, Sister. No one will be out tonight. You can take that to the bank."

She smiled at Sister Alicia, who returned the smile as she rolled out a tarp and blankets beside the girls.

"How is the arm?"

I leaned back against my saddle. "Okay. Still hurts, but not as bad."

Sister Rossetta nodded to my saddlebags. "Perhaps some of the whiskey would help. Do you believe so?"

Surprised, I sat up.

She laughed. "I could not help seeing when you placed it in the saddlebags back at the mission. I think that probably some in your coffee will warm you from the rain and perhaps ease the pain in your arm. Yes?"

I chuckled. "Sister, for a nun, you know the way to a man's heart." I lost no time in fishing the bottle from the bags and pouring a generous slug of whiskey into my coffee.

"I wasn't always a nun, Mr. Burnett."

I sipped the spiked coffee and groaned in satisfaction. I leaned back against the saddle, enjoying the heat of the fire on the soles of my boots. The wind snapped and fluttered the tarps. "How long you been in the nun business, Sister?"

She gave me a sly look. "A long time, Mr. Burnett. Since I was fifteen." Her eyes twinkled in merriment.

I reckon women are women even if they do wear a black habit. She had neatly crowhopped over her age. I nodded to the girls, who were snuggled down in their soogan. "It's hard to believe you're going all this way after gold, Sister Rossetta."

Sister Alicia lay beside the girls.

Outside, the rain slammed against the canvas. The

walls moved in and out. "Perhaps, but that's what the Holy Father St. Matthew wishes."

"How do you know where you're going? I mean, where to find the gold?"

"Oh, we have directions. Otherwise, we would never have attempted the journey."

"Directions? You mean a waybill, a map?" Something seemed far out of kilter.

"Not a map, but very explicit directions from Father Kino, the priest who buried the gold in Black Mountain."

She had mentioned the mountain before, a few nights earlier when she also announced that St. Matthew had sent me. "I've traipsed around Austin some, Sister, but I never saw any mountains. Some hills, but nothing that I would call a mountain."

Her smile faded. "So I have been told by others. You see, Father Kino was a very dedicated priest who lived in the desert along the Rio Bravo all his life. He had never seen mountains, only the desert. To him, one of your hills might have been a mountain."

"What was he doing in that part of the country anyway?"

"The church sent him to Nacogdoches with gold to establish some missions. Comanches attacked, and the story goes that Father Kino led the train away from the Spanish Trail for several days in an effort to escape. They buried the gold. All died on the return trip except two nuns."

"And they brought with them a waybill, I suppose." I arched an eyebrow.

She frowned. "A waybill?"

I nodded. "Yes. Instructions. Directions."

"Oh. Oh yes. Naturally." From within her habit,

she pulled out a leather packet and fished out a folded sheet of paper. She opened it and offered it to me. "This is a copy—what you called a waybill."

I held it to the firelight. It was written in Spanish. I shook my head and handed it back to her. "I know a little of the Mex lingo, Sister, but this is beyond me."

With a knowing smile, she took the waybill and held it to the firelight. She translated slowly.

"In the middle of the Black Mountains is a very rough pass in which there exists a cave of bees. Once through the pass, a horseshoe bend in the Colorado River is plainly seen. On the east side of the bend is a sheer bluff of limestone facing west. On the south slope of the bluff is a tunnel behind a boulder. The rock with the visage of a demon looks at the gold."

She looked up. While she spoke, she folded the page and returned it to the pouch. "The nuns claim Father Kino led all fifteen burros into the tunnel. He was absent for many hours. He returned without the burros. Each animal carried one hundred pounds of gold bars."

I choked on the coffee and whiskey. "One . . . hundred pounds? Fifteen of them?"

She nodded. "Now you can see just how important it is to us. With that gold, we can build a hospital and school for the unfortunate."

With that much gold, she could build a dozen hospitals and schools for the unfortunate. I studied her for several moments. I couldn't help admire her dedication to her church. "You think the gold is still there? I'd wager a sum that more than one jasper has read those directions."

"And you would lose, Mr. Burnett," she replied

with a calm assurance that surprised me. "You see, my great-great grandmother's sister was one of the two surviving nuns. Upon reaching Cerralvo and telling their story, they were instructed to set the directions on paper. Her sister nun was unable to read or write, so the task was given to my great-great-great aunt. As she did so, she was visited that night by a stranger who made her a generous offer to reveal the secret. Realizing the greed that sought the gold, she neglected important details in the paper she gave the church. She kept the accurate description until she could be certain the church would take possession of the gold."

"And now is the time, huh? Two nuns and two girls." I shook my head. "Seems mighty odd you and Sister Alicia taking a couple girls with you on this gold hunt."

She and Sister Alicia exchanged looks. "The girls are going to a new home. Mary Elizabeth's family was drowned in a storm off the coast. She was the only survivor. After almost two years, we found distant relatives near the village of Bastrop. They have agreed to take Mary Elizabeth and Carmaline, who is also an orphan."

I downed the rest of my spiked coffee. "Well, Sister, I've got to admit, you sure did cut off a big chunk of trouble to chew on."

She rose and in a crouch stepped over the girls and lay on the blanket next to Sister Alicia, propping herself on one elbow. She smiled. "That's why the Holy Father St. Matthew sent you to us, Mr. Burnett." With those words, she lay back and closed her eyes. "Good night, Mr. Burnett. Don't forget to say your prayers."

I stared gape-mouthed at her, amazed at her simple

conviction. If I'd possessed that much assurance ten
years earlier, I would be the cattle king of Texas by
now instead of a wet, down-at-the-heels cowpoke
knocking around the countryside.

She was confident. I had to give her that, but she
was sorely mistaken if she thought I was going to
nursemaid them up to Bastrop and then on to Austin.
Cuero was as far as I was going, unless the Comancheros decided to continue north. But there was no
reason for them to head north. They'd likely angle
northwest toward San Antonio after selling their
plunder.

"Don't count on it, Sister Rossetta," I said above
the soft crackling of the fire. "I'm after those who
killed my partner." I popped the cork on the whiskey
bottle and splashed another dollop of Monongalhela
Whiskey in my cup.

Sister Rossetta's eyes remained closed, but a grin
curled the edge of her lips.

The fire had died when I awakened, and a chill had
filled the tent. The girls and the sisters were bundled
in the blankets.

Silently, I stirred the coals and fed tinder to the
small flames. I worked the coffeepot into the edge of
the coals. I sat back and flexed the fingers of my right
hand, clenching my teeth against the shots of pain. My
arm was healing quickly, but not as quickly as I
wanted.

Outside, the rain continued to fall. By now, it had
shifted from out of the east, which meant the storm
was directly south of us. Hard to say how far, though.
Some of those storms that howl in off the Gulf of
Mexico are three, four hundred miles across. Best I

could figure, at the speed it was moving, we'd be stuck here another night at least.

I peered through the sheeting rain. A sheen of water lay over the ground as far as I could see. Bands of silver rain drove into the water, creating what looked like thousands of tiny explosions.

Donning my poncho and pulling my hat down over my ears, I stomped out into the mud to check the animals. They stood hipshot under the canopy of limbs and leaves, wet and bedraggled. I moved them a few feet into some fresh graze. I wished I could have found a spot out of the weather, but that was impossible. We'd all suffer together.

Back in the tent, breakfast bubbled over the fire. About the best that could be said about it was that it was hot. I was tired of chewing on soup and stew. I wanted to sink my teeth in something solid. I glanced at the sidearm on my hip: an old Colt Navy. Chances for a solid meal were slim.

The rain continued throughout the day, gradually shifting to the west, which indicated the storm had passed and the rain would soon cease.

That night, a few stars peeked through the clouds.

With the storm moving away from us, I should have relaxed, but I couldn't. If I wasn't mistaken, we had two rivers to cross before Cuero. And with the catawampus amount of rain the storm had brought, they were bound to be overflowing.

I couldn't sleep much that night.

Chapter Six

We reached Coleto Creek just before noon. Cascading toward the Gulf, the storm had turned the placid little stream into a churning, roiling flood that threatened to overflow its banks. Tangles of dead and uprooted timber swirled with the current, their branches whipping the water into a foam that resembled piles of dirty cotton. From time to time, pieces of the foam broke away from the debris and, caught up in the current, sped on downstream.

I sat on the chestnut, staring at the muddy water almost thirty yards across. Both girls stood at the river's edge. "Not too close, girls," I said, failing to notice just how much the twisting current was eating into the sandy bank. I was too busy cursing to myself. Every moment of delay put me farther behind the Comancheros. If I had been alone, I'd chance the creek, but I had promised to see the sisters and the girls to Cuero. That's what I got for being so soft hearted. I glanced back at Sister Rossetta. "Too

43

chancy to cross here, Sister. We got no ropes. The current will sweep the buckboard downstream . . . the animals with it.''

She nodded. "So what do you suggest, Mr. Burnett?''

Before I could answer, the girls screamed. I jerked around in time to see Carmaline leap backward as the sandy bank caved in, taking Mary Elizabeth with it into the flooding river.

I jerked the chestnut around and dug my heels into his flanks. He balked, rearing on the legs and pawing at the sky. I glanced around his neck. The little blond girl was nowhere to be seen.

Jerking the reins savagely, I yanked the frightened horse's head around, spinning him and then driving him toward the water again. And again he balked.

I leaped from the saddle. Several feet from shore, Mary Elizabeth sputtered to the surface. Wrenching my arm from its sling, I threw off my hat and did a belly flop into the muddy water. I wasn't much of a swimmer, but in four or five strokes I reached the screaming youngster.

She climbed all over me, driving us both underwater. I wrapped my good arm around her waist and kicked toward shore, or at least in the direction I thought the shore to be.

We popped out of the water, coughing and choking. Mary Elizabeth tried to turn so she could grasp me, but I maintained my hold on her, pulling her tightly against my side. Awkwardly, I struggled toward shore. Suddenly, my feet touched bottom.

The sisters waded into the waist-deep water. Sister Rossetta grabbed Mary Elizabeth, and Sister Alicia seized my arm, supporting me while I staggered from the churning water.

I sagged to the ground exhausted. Now that the emergency was over, my arm began throbbing. Moments later, Sister Alicia was holding out a tin cup, half full of Monongalhela Whiskey.

Gently, she slipped my arm back into the sling while I gratefully sipped the whiskey.

We camped in a nearby patch of oak and pecan. By mid-afternoon, I felt better. Mary Elizabeth acted as if nothing had happened. She and Carmaline were busy with their catechisms, the sisters with their prayers.

I decided to get some meat.

Game was plentiful. But there was a problem. I was a terrible shot. The only way I would have chanced a shot with my left hand was if I stood less than ten feet from my target.

The animals must have known I was a lousy shot, for they stood watching me, well within rifle range but too distant for my skill with a handgun. Deer stood in the shade of the pecan and oak, staring at me, just out of range. Wild hogs snorted at me, just out of range.

After about an hour, I gave up and headed back.

That's when I spotted the chicken. A white leghorn pecking at the ground near the shoreline. I reined up, suddenly wary. Was there a cabin around? I saw nothing.

Several yards downstream, I spotted what appeared to be the tangled wreckage of a shed. In the middle of the debris was a roosting ladder.

"So that's what it's all about," I muttered, eyeing the chicken hungrily. The flood upriver swept the shed away, and the leghorn hitched a ride to stay out of the water.

I remained motionless in the saddle and studied the chicken. No way could I run her down. When it comes to twisting and darting, chickens are right up there with cats.

Easing the chestnut back, I dismounted and tied him to a mesquite. Then I started searching for the right limb, thumb-sized, five to six feet long, with a backward hook at the end, like a V.

More than once as a youngster, I kept such a tool whittled and leaning in the corner of the cabin for whenever ma had me run down a chicken for Sunday dinner. It wasn't often, for the chickens provided eggs and more chickens. But when one stopped laying, I headed for the chicken tool and the poor hen was headed for the table.

Chickens will tolerate a person to within three feet or so. Any closer, they skedaddle faster than skeeters after blood. But with my chicken tool, you slip the hook around a leg. When the chicken tries to pull away, he wedges his leg more tightly in the V.

My chicken tool worked perfectly. The first try, I snagged one. I killed the chicken before returning to camp, figuring the sisters and the girls would prove squeamish if I throttled the chicken in front of them and let it flop about on the ground.

We didn't have any fat, so we couldn't fry it. We roasted it, and everyone ate his and her fill.

Next morning, Coleto Creek had dropped enough for us to cross and continue our journey. Ten miles or so ahead was the Guadalupe River.

We reached it by mid-afternoon.

The river was twice the width of Coleto Creek. I studied our predicament. We might have to wait a week for the river to drop. Too long.

"Problems, Mr. Burnett?"

I glanced over my shoulder at the ladies in the buckboard. All four watched me expectantly. "Looks that way, sister. Cuero's on the other side of the river."

Sister Alicia and the two girls peered across the muddy water coursing downstream. I grinned to myself when I saw that Mary Elizabeth and Carmaline remained in the buckboard, well away from the riverbank.

Sister Rossetta gave a half shrug and smiled. "That's all right. We can just continue north along the river. Somewhere up ahead, we should be able to cross."

I didn't know if nuns were supposed to be hardheaded or not, but Sister Rossetta could give lessons on how to be mule stubborn to that longhorn cow that busted my arm. Patiently, I said, "Now, Sister, I told you before. I'm not taking you to Austin. I've got to get into Cuero to see if anyone spotted those Comancheros. That's the likely spot they would have sold the cattle they stole from me and my partner."

For some reason I couldn't quite put my finger on, I winced at the disappointment on Sister Alicia's and the girls' faces. Sister Rossetta simply continued smiling. "Then we'll wait right here until you return, Mr. Burnett." She climbed off the buckboard. "Come, girls. Let's set up camp. In that cluster of cottonwoods over there." She pointed to a stand of trees on a sand and gravel rise several yards from shore.

"But Sister . . ." I hesitated. Maybe she had the right idea. "Okay, Sister. Let's set up camp. Then I'll send someone out from Cuero to look after you. How's that?"

She gave me a quick wink. "You'll be back, Mr. Burnett. You'll see."

That woman was exasperating. Arguing with her was like bucking the tiger in Dodge City. No way to win. With a sigh, I dismounted and helped set up camp. "Like I said, when I get to Cuero, I'll send someone back for you. Maybe you can talk him into taking you on to Austin."

She just gave me another one of those funny-looking smiles.

They all stood watching from the bank as I swam the chestnut across. I clambered out on the far side, about two hundred yards downriver. The sisters and the girls were standing by the buckboard, staring at me. I felt a tinge of regret but dismissed it. I gave them a wave and turned my pony toward Cuero. And the Comancheros.

Within a mile of the river, I ran into the first trail herd. Cal Raines was the trail boss for the Four Circle. He was ready to move the herd out, having bought the last cattle that morning.

Wrinkles carved deep war trails in his sun-browned skin. "Nope. Ain't seen no one like you described." He gave a short nod toward the village. "Jobe Hazlip has his herd about a mile or so thataway. Maybe he saw something."

Hazlip was no help, so I rode on into Cuero. On the edge of the village, a withered old Mexican woman squatted before a fire in front of a wickiup of sticks and mud. The tiny village was no better, its buildings fashioned of adobe and sticks. Like most small hamlets, the saloon and the dry goods store were the most prosperous-appearing. I searched for a church, figuring on help from the priest in finding someone who would look after the children and the sisters.

I saw nothing that looked like a church. I pulled up at the saloon and dragged my tongue over my lips. I had three dollars and about a third of a bottle left in my saddlebags. I could do without a drink this time. All I needed was information.

The Comancheros had been in Cuero. The topic of conversation in the saloon was the murder of a family east of town and the pursuit of the killers through the chaparral before losing them when the Mexican outlaws crossed the Guadalupe.

The hombre telling the story paused, leaned back against the plank and barrel bar, and eyed the dozen or so townspeople in the saloon. A shock of red hair stuck out from under his hat. "They stopped us at the river. Hid out in the willows on the far side and pot-shotted us." He downed a slug of whiskey. "They would have got us sure if we'd gone into the river. Figured we'd let the sheriff go after them."

Someone snorted. "Cass? Not in your lifetime."

A round of chuckles greeted the snide remark.

I cleared my throat. "You sure it was Comancheros, mister?"

He cut his eyes at me, suspicion wrinkling his forehead. "Who might you be, stranger? I ain't never seen you around here."

"Just rode in." I glanced at the curious faces watching me. "I been chasing Comancheros. Two killed my partner back on the Mission River this side of Refugio. Stole our stock. Robbed us blind.''

Red looked me up and down. His lips twisted in a sneer. "Don't look like you could do much, should you find them."

A few chuckles came from the onlookers. I laughed with them. "Don't let looks fool you, mister." The smile faded from my face. My voice grew cold. "I'm like a bulldog. I get my teeth in your throat, you'll have to kill me before I turn loose."

The sneer faded from his lips. He cleared his throat.

I stared at him. "Were you there? At the river?"

"Yeah. Yeah, I was there."

I gestured to my waist. "One wore a sash, red and yellow. If you saw them, you had to see something that bright."

His eyes grew wide. "By jasper, that was them. The one with the red and yellow sash. He was there. Big hombre. Belly that looked like a pumpkin."

My blood grew hot with excitement. "Where did they cross the river?"

Red pointed a long arm to the north. "Five or six miles up where the river cuts straight back east. Can't miss it." He paused. "But they didn't have no cattle or horses. You say they stole yours?" He nodded to my arm. "They do that to you?"

"No." I grinned crookedly. "A plug-ugly mean longhorn gave me this. My partner and I were popping them out of the brush."

The crowd laughed, and the bartender splashed some whiskey into a glass. "Here you go, stranger. You look like you could use a drink."

I ignored the bartender. I turned to Red. "When was

this? I mean, when did you boys chase them across the river?''

''Yesterday. Just before noon.''

The bartender shoved the tumbler of whiskey in front of me. ''Drink up, stranger.''

Red held up his glass. ''Here's to you, stranger. Hope you catch them two.''

I made up my mind in a hurry. Even while the whiskey was sloshing down my gullet, burning into my stomach, I decided to find someone to look after the sisters while I pushed on ahead. I was too close to the Comancheros to play nursemaid. ''This town got a preacher or a priest?''

Red snickered. ''You don't look like a praying sort to me.''

''I ain't. My ma tried to teach me right, but I was mighty wild.''

The bartender spoke up. ''There's a preacher on the north end of town. He lives above the livery. They use the barn for services.''

I thanked him. I surveyed the men in the saloon. I didn't figure any of them would be interested in helping the sisters, but I decided to ask anyway. All they could say was no. ''By the way, there's a couple nuns on the other side of Guadalupe, aiming for Bastrop and then Austin. Anyone here be interested in escorting them?''

No one replied.

Then a voice from a back table asked, ''What are they paying?''

I chuckled. ''Good company and their thanks.''

''No money?''

''No, sir.''

A few snickers made the rounds. Red shook his

head. "Not me. My time is too valuable to run off to Austin with a couple nuns."

The bartender sneered. "Yeah. That means you'd have to give up your afternoon and evenings in here."

The room laughed at Red's expense.

The preacher lived above the livery, his room one of two at the top of a flight of stairs with a broken railing. George Adam Brownlee, with thin hair plastered across his bald head, was an itinerant preacher who, in a stroke of lightning, realized the call of God. Best I could figure, he wasn't of any particular denomination. "Just the Bible, my son," he proclaimed solemnly. "God Almighty just wants His children to love Him."

I glanced around the peanut-sized room. A wooden bunk took up one wall, a desk and chair another, a window and a rack of clothes the third.

He offered me his chair. "Thanks, preacher. But this won't take long." I told him the story, leaving out their quest for the gold. "I hate like the blazes to leave the sisters alone, but those outlaws are only about twenty-four hours ahead. If you or someone you know will take the sisters and children on to Bastrop and then Austin, I'll stop back in and pay them twenty-five dollars from my own pocket."

"Such a lengthy journey just to return an orphan to her family is curious, very curious. Why couldn't they have simply sent the two girls by stage?"

I hesitated. I hated to lie, so I just pleaded ignorance. "Beats me, parson. They want to get to Austin, and I feel obligated since they helped me out of a bind." I held up my bandaged arm. "I'd like to see them well took care of."

He shook his head. "I wish I could help, Mr. Burnett. My obligations demand my presence here, and I think from what you said, the gentlemen at the saloon gave you their answer."

I grimaced and cursed under my breath. I should have known. Yet there were no second guesses because there were no choices for me. I had to stay with the sisters. Then another thought struck me. What if I brought them into Cuero and left them?

Instantly, I knew the answer to that question. Sister Rossetta would simply continue from Cuero.

Reluctantly, I departed. As I left his room, I spotted the hostler heading down the stairs ahead of me on his bowed legs. "Hey, mister."

He jerked around, his eyes wide. "W-what?"

I guess he hadn't heard me behind him, and I startled him. "I need some rope. You got a couple lariats right cheap?"

He gulped. He glanced nervously at the preacher's room, then nodded. "Y-yeah. Yeah, I think I got a couple around here." He hurried into the tack room. I glanced up the stairs. The door to his room was open a crack. Had he been listening? If so, what could he have heard that made him so nervous?

Abruptly, he returned with two lariats, both well used but still serviceable. I paid him a dollar and rode out, heading back for the Guadalupe.

Chapter Seven

The sun was an angry red behind the cottonwood and pecan lining the Guadalupe River when I pulled up at the shore where I had clambered out earlier in the day. The current was still swift. I peered upriver at the stand of cottonwoods where we had made camp.

"What the . . . !" The camp had vanished.

I rubbed my fist into my eyes and looked again.

Nothing.

I looked upriver and down. Was I in the right spot? I had to be. The ground at my feet was torn and scarred from the hooves of my chestnut scrambling from the river this morning.

A cold chill ran up my back. Comancheros!

I dug my heels into the chestnut and drove the animal into swift water. Weary from a day's riding, he struggled against the current. I slipped from the saddle and, hooking my injured arm about the horn, swam beside the animal. Together, we made it across.

Quickly, I swung back into the saddle and urged him into a gallop.

Scattered ashes and faint impressions in the thin sand and gravel of the buckboard's butcher-knife wheels heading north were the only evidence the camp had ever existed.

A cold hand clutched my heart. No way Sister Rossetta would have left without me. She was so muleheaded-certain I would return that the only thing that could have moved her was a one-in-a-hundred-years' flood.

Or the Comancheros.

Shucking my six-gun, I studied the sign, casting to the left or right for indications of accompanying horses. What the blazes was going on? What could have prodded Sister Rossetta to move out? With a click of my tongue, I headed up the trail.

Suddenly, a branch flew through the air. My chestnut shied, and I almost lost my seat. "Whoa, there, blast you! Whoa!"

I jerked around. My eyes bulged.

Emerging from a thicket of briars was Carmaline, Mary Elizabeth, and Sister Alicia, who motioned frantically at me. "Over here, Mr. Burrnett, over here."

Alarmed, I glanced around but spotted nothing. Quickly, I dug my heels into the chestnut's flanks and headed him for the underbrush. Carmaline led the way through the briars and willows into a tangle of grapevines smothering a dead elm.

I dismounted and tied my chestnut to a willow. The tangle of grapevines had formed a teepee over the elm, leaving an open area around the trunk. It was a cozy little room.

They stared up at me. Despite the deepening shadows of the evening, I saw the fear in their eyes. "What's going on? Where's Sister Rossetta?"

All three started jabbering at once. I held up my hands. "Slow down. You're gobbling like a flock of turkeys. One at a time. Now, Sister Alicia, you tell me. What happened?"

She chewed on her bottom lip and took a deep breath, trying to still her excitement. "Comancheros, Mr. Burnett. We saw the Comancheros. At least, that's what we guessed they were. Anyway, Sister Rossetta made us hide, and then she drove on north, trying to lead them away from us."

I gaped at the sister. "She did what?"

The girls nodded vigorously. "They were real ugly, too, Mr. Burnett," Mary Elizabeth blurted out. "We put out the fire when we saw them."

Carmaline interrupted. "Sister Rossetta hid us in here before she left. Just a few minutes later, the Comancheros rode past."

Mary Elizabeth hugged herself and leaned against my leg. "I was scared."

I laid my hand on her shoulder. "Hold on, hold on. You're safe now." I looked at Sister Alicia. "But you got me confused. What do you mean, you put out the fire when you saw them?"

Taking a deep breath to still her nervousness, Sister Alicia explained. "We were sitting by the fire when we spotted them across the river. They didn't see us, but Sister Rossetta figured they would smell the wood smoke and come back. We broke camp, hid here, and

Sister took the buckboard north to lead them away if they came back.''

''Did they?'' I glanced at the girls before turning my attention back to Sister Alicia.

''Yes. About ten minutes later. Wouldn't you say so, girls?'' Sister Alicia looked at the two youngsters.

They nodded emphatically.

I studied them a moment, trying to plan my next step. ''How long ago did all this take place?''

Alicia chewed on her lip. ''About an hour. Maybe a little longer.''

An hour. Too long for anyone to be at the mercy of Comancheros. ''Look, you stay here. I'll go after Sister Rossetta.'' I unsheathed my knife and offered it to Sister Alicia. ''This is all I have if they return.''

With a mischievous grin, Sister Alicia raised the hem of her black habit. My cheeks burned, and I started to turn around, but she stopped me. ''I'm not who you think I am, Mr. Burnett.'' She pulled a small revolver from her boot and held it up. ''That's all right, Mr. Burnett. I have this.''

I gaped at the handgun.

''It's a Remington derringer. Forty-one caliber.''

Before I could stammer out a single word, she pushed the habit from her head, revealing a tumble of dark hair. She slipped out of the habit. ''I'm not a nun. My name is Alicia Wells. I have an aunt in Austin who Sister Rossetta was taking me to. She figured I'd have less problems with people along the way if they thought I was a nun.''

The girls giggled. Obviously, they had known all along. I was speechless. On the one hand, I felt like a foolish clodhopper, but on the other, I felt like whistling a tune. I couldn't understand why my feelings were so mixed, but now wasn't the time to try to sort them.

I studied her. She wore a dark denim shirt that was wrinkled and a skirt split down the middle with the legs sewn together. I finally managed to nod. ''That makes sense, but like I said, you stay here. I'm riding after the sister.'' I looked Alicia up and down. ''You best put the habit back on. You're better off a nun out here in the wilderness.''

I looked around the interior of their refuge. Layer after layer of decades-old grapevines formed an almost impenetrable shelter. I added, ''You sit tight in here. Impossible for anybody to see you from outside, but no fire.'' I looked directly at Carmaline and Mary Elizabeth. ''You girls are going to be just fine, you hear?''

Carmaline nodded. ''I'm not scared now that you're here, Mr. Burnett.''

I hesitated, momentarily flustered by the girl's admission. I glanced at Alicia who smiled grimly. I cleared my throat. ''Just stay inside. I'll be back.''

I led the chestnut from the underbrush and swung into the saddle. Moments later, I picked up the trail of the buckboard, but if the Comancheros were following Sister Rossetta, I couldn't tell.

A few hundred yards north, I reached a strip of damp, hard-packed sand. I reined up and grimaced. Despite the lengthening shadows, I could read the message it carried. The wheels cut deeply into the sand as did the wide-spaced hoof prints indicating the animals were running. I cast about. Toward the river, I found the sign of two horses. One glance at the depth and angle of the tracks in the sand told me the animals were in a gallop.

Not even an Apache can determine the age of tracks

in loose sand. But I figured I was staring at the tracks made by the Comancheros.

By now, the sun had dropped below the horizon, leaving behind a sheen of red across the sky that bathed the river bank in a bloody cloak. I rode cautiously, sniffing the air, guessing the Comancheros might chance a fire, especially if they had Sister Rossetta. The only problem with the swirling breezes along the river was the thick undergrowth and animal trails that funneled the wind in every direction. If I caught a trace of wood smoke, their animals might catch a scent of me.

The river made a wide curve to the west. I remained at the edge of the underbrush, ready to duck into its heavy foliage if I spotted them ahead.

A whiff of wood smoke teased my nostrils. I stiffened, peering ahead into the growing dusk, hoping for a glimpse of firelight.

Nothing.

I dismounted and tied my pony to a willow. Slowly, I eased north, staying close to the undergrowth. The acrid odor of wood smoke grew stronger.

Suddenly, there it was: a flicker of light through the tangled leaves and vines. I dropped to a knee and waited, expecting to hear the whinny of their horses when the animals picked up my smell.

Long moments passed. In a crouch, I scurried across the open area between the treeline and the river's edge, where I ducked below the bank and stood ankle deep in water. By now, dusk had settled and the stars were beginning to pop out.

I moved upriver. The flicker of firelight grew brighter. I froze. Silhouetted between me and the fire were their two horses, grazing contentedly. Off to the right, I made out the shadowy outline of the buck-board, the white and bay still in the traces.

The Comancheros knew what they were doing. They had made their camp in the undergrowth, where any approach was made difficult by the thick chaparral. From time to time, shadows moved in front of the fire.

Carefully, I moved north of the camp, hoping to stay on the downwind side of the horses. An old elm, its trunk almost two feet in diameter, stood in the midst of a briar patch some fifty yards from the camp. About twenty feet up, limbs were missing on the south side, offering a clear view of the camp from that position.

Holstering my six-gun, I fastened the rawhide loop over the hammer and favoring my healing arm, started climbing, keeping the trunk between myself and the camp.

When I reached the opening, I pressed against the trunk. The rough bark dug into my cheek as I peered down at the camp. The fire was low. Despite the shadows, I spotted Sister Rossetta. She was leaning against the trunk of a willow. The shadows were too thick to be certain, but she held herself as if she were tied.

The two Comancheros sprawled against their saddles on one side of the fire, laughing and arguing and passing the bottle between them. I wished for my Brass Boy Henry, a .44 caliber lever action with a fifteen-shot magazine. With it, I could have picked the Comancheros off as easy as stomping cockroaches.

All I had was my .36 caliber Colt Navy sidegun. I had to get closer, much closer. But how? I couldn't forget the horses.

I eased back down the elm and leaned back against

the trunk. I had to wait until the outlaws slept. Then I'd make my move.

The fire burned low. From the position of the Big Dipper, I figured it was a couple hours after midnight. For the last few hours, I had peered into the shadows around me, planning my course of action. I decided to circle the camp, putting the sleeping men between me and the horses. I rose slowly, easing through the briars and wild huckleberries. The limbs scratched against my clothes, but I continued moving, one slow step at a time.

One of their ponies whinnied. I froze, my ears straining for any sound from camp. I heard nothing. I continued.

It took two hours to travel less than seventy-five yards, but finally I was lying on my belly beneath a tangle of woody greenbrier less than twenty feet from the camp.

No more than ten feet distant, Sister Rossetta had her back to me, her hands tied behind the trunk of the small mesquite. She was awake, for I could see her hands twisting and struggling with her bonds. Beyond her, the two outlaws snored.

Silently, I crawled up behind her. I whispered, "Sister."

She froze.

"It's me, Jack Burnett. Be still. I'll cut you loose."

Her answer was to stretch the bonds around her wrists.

I added, "Don't move until I say so, then roll into the underbrush." I laid my handgun on the ground, unsheathed my knife, and sliced through the ropes cutting into her wrists. I picked up my revolver and rose to my knees. I leaned forward. "Get ready."

Silently, I stood.

At that moment, a horse whinnied, and the Comanchero nearest opened his eyes. We stared at each other a moment, both surprised. "Now," I yelled at the sister, while squeezing off a shot as the Comanchero shouted and tried to jump to his feet.

My slug caught him in the chest and knocked him back into the second Comanchero, the one with the big belly and bright sash. Awkwardly, I cocked my revolver with my left hand and fired again. Three feet from the Comancheros, the fire exploded from my slug.

Off to my left, the horses squealed and tore at the underbrush with their hooves, frantically trying to escape the commotion.

I cursed and cocked the hammer and fired again.

The first Comanchero jerked as the slug hit him. His compadre rolled into the underbrush and leaped to his feet. I fired again, but all I heard was the crashing of underbrush as the fleeing outlaw tried to put as much distance between us as he could. I fired a last slug into the brush after the retreating sounds. Quickly, I reloaded and looked around for Sister Rossetta.

A snort and squeal jerked me around. I leaped aside as the Comanchero's frightened ponies raced through the camp and disappeared into the night.

I rolled to my feet. "Sister Rossetta, where are you?"

A tiny voice came from the underbrush. "Are they gone?"

I looked at the outlaw on the ground at my feet.

"Come on out, Sister. He's gone. This one won't hurt you. We lost their horses."

She appeared from the darkness. "Are you all right, Mr. Burnett?"

"Don't worry about me, Sister. What about you? They hurt you?"

She halted and looked up at me. "Come morning, they would have." She cut her eyes downriver. "Where are the girls?"

"They're fine. Don't worry." I surveyed the camp, grinning when I spotted holsters and six-guns draped over the Comancheros' saddles. I found four saddle guns, counting McKeever's Winchester and my Brass Boy Henry. I cocked a cartridge into the chamber and handed the rifle to the sister. "Here," I said.

Her eyes grew wide as I picked up their sidearms. "What are you doing?"

"Why, I'm taking their gear, that's what."

"But that's robbing the dead, Mr. Burnett."

I hesitated. "Look, Sister, if I don't take them, someone else will. Besides, up the road we might be able to do some trading." I nodded toward the rifle in her hand. "Now you keep an eye out for that other owlhoot while I load this gear into the buckboard. Then we're lighting a shuck out of here."

With a terse nod, she agreed. She glanced at the rifle. Worried, she said. "I can't shoot him, you know, Mr. Burnett."

"I know, Sister. But you can shoot at the ground in front of him, can't you?"

She studied the question a moment. "Yes, I can do that."

While she stood guard, I threw the saddles, rifles, and grub in the buckboard. I tossed the outlaws' soogans in the fire, not wanting to put up with the ticks and lice in their blankets. Before leaving, I went through the dead Comanchero's pockets. He had about fifty dollars, which I claimed as compensation for the theft of our cattle.

"Ready?" I looked up at Sister Rossetta.

A frown knit her face. "Aren't you going to bury him?"

"Bury him? Sister, we don't have the time."

She nodded. "Yes we do, Mr. Burnett. I'll stand guard with this rifle while you take care of him. After all, he was one of God's children gone astray."

I was tempted to throw her in the buckboard bodily, but I didn't. As usual, she got her way. Fortunately, the ground was sandy, and it only took an hour to scrape out a hole for him. I pushed the last of the sand over him and looked around at the sister. "Satisfied?"

"Yes. Now we can go."

Wiping the sweat from my forehead, I helped Sister Rossetta in the buckboard. "You drive, Sister." I sat beside her and cocked my Henry. "I don't know if the one who got away has a sidearm or not, but I'll keep watch just to be on the safe side."

We picked up my chestnut and within fifteen minutes reached the girls who were huddled beneath the vine-smothered elm. Quickly, we loaded them in the wagon and turned north.

I didn't know what was ahead of us, but I sure as blazes knew what was behind.

Chapter Eight

The night was clear, the stars bright. We made slow time, but we kept moving. The only sound was the jangling of the O-rings, the grunt of the ponies, and the squeak of leather punctuated by the occasional clatter of the iron rim against rock.

At dawn, we pulled up for a fast breakfast. I'd been used to seeing two nuns busying themselves around the camp. Now one of the nuns turned out to be a right pretty young lady with a mighty attractive smile. While I sipped my coffee, I listened to Alicia Wells's story.

"Then what about the gold, Sister Rossetta. Was that just a make-believe story too?"

"Oh no, Mr. Burnett. The gold is there." She nodded to Alicia. "I tried to get help back in Indianola, but they just scoffed at me about the gold. Then Alicia told me of her cousin in Austin. He's a young man she believes we can trust. He can put together a small party of dependable and reliable individuals to help us.''

She continued talking about their hopes and dreams, but I didn't pay too much attention. I was too busy looking at Alicia Wells and letting my imagination run away with me. Of course, a rundown cowpoke like me had nothing to offer her—or any woman. I certainly wouldn't have someone like her live in a ramshackle shack while I wrangled for a big rancher for thirty dollars a month. A fine woman like Alicia Wells deserved more than that.

Finally, we broke camp. I threw a saddle on the chestnut and rode beside the buckboard. Sister Rossetta looked up at me. ''You think the Comanchero is following us?''

I frowned. ''Hard to say. Usually, his kind take to the woods like a spooked coyote. But we're best off if we keep a sharp eye.''

The next four days passed without incident. We crossed the Guadalupe near Gonzales. By then, I was fairly certain the Comanchero had dragged his worthless carcass back to Mexico. I'd met and worked with a heap of folks from Mexico, and for the most part they were honest, good people, like the majority of us here in Texas. But every place has those who try to take what someone else has worked hard to acquire.

Maybe the Federales would catch Big Belly when he crossed the Rio Grande. Still, I didn't like the uncertainty of not knowing.

That night, on the bank of the Guadalupe, I lay in my soogan staring at the stars, trying to decide my next step. I had McKeever's and my gear back, and one of the Comancheros was dead. I had a choice now.

I could leave the sister and her wards and head south, hoping to pick up the trail of the last Comanchero—a task just about as impossible as swallowing a horned toad backwards—or forwards for that matter.

Time and again, I had sworn to Sister Rossetta I was not going to Austin. With a wry grin, I knew if I changed my mind, I'd have to eat crow. But like my pa always told me, "Boy, if you got to eat crow, eat it while it's warm. It's a whole lot harder to swallow when it gets cold."

Might as well eat it now. Without moving, I said, "You asleep, Sister?"

Her soft but firm voice came from the other side of the fire. "No. Is something wrong, Mr. Burnett?"

I hesitated. "No, I just thought I'd let you know that I decided I'll take you on to Bastrop and Austin."

Instead of thanking me or sounding pleased, she simply replied matter of factly. "I knew you would do so, Mr. Burnett. Didn't I tell you?"

I turned my head and glanced at her, but I couldn't resist grinning. I'd met a heap of strong ladies in my life, and Sister Rossetta ranked right up there with the best of them. "Yeah, Sister, I reckon you did." I chuckled.

"Something funny, Mr. Burnett?" She turned to look across the fire at me.

"No, Sister, not a thing." I turned over and promptly dropped off to sleep.

The next few days to Bastrop was right pleasant despite the heat. The truth was, I enjoyed the journey. The countryside was rolling with hills of oak and juniper. We met a few riders coming and going on the road, a daily stage, and a couple snake-oil salesmen.

Game was plentiful. With my Brass Boy Henry, I brought in venison, which we roasted, baked, and broiled. The trip was a happy one. Sister Rossetta kept them all singing gay little tunes like "The Flying Trapeze" and the lighthearted ditty sung by Southern soldiers named "Goober Peas." Our voices echoed down the lush valleys and over the rolling hills.

I was tone deaf, for I never could stay on key. We all laughed at my miserable singing, but it was friendly laughter. Like a family.

One morning, we pulled up on a hill and peered north. There, nestled in the giant cottonwoods and oaks on the banks of the Colorado River, lay Bastrop. Off to our right was a stand of pines, the Lost Pines of Texas, a unique stand of loblollies almost a hundred miles west of the main pine belt in the state.

"Well, Sister, there's Bastrop." I nodded to the small village, surprised to realize I wasn't anxious for the trip to end even though we had another thirty miles after Bastrop. It doesn't take a genius to pick a goat out of a heard of sheep, and it didn't take a genius to know why I didn't want the journey to end. I liked being around the ladies. All of them, but especially Alicia.

My ears burned when I thought about her. But I was a dirt-poor cowpoke whose prospects would make any jasper hang up his fiddle. I had nothing to offer a pretty young filly like Alicia Wells, so the smartest move I could make was to forget about her.

We hit the main road into town, which at one time, according to my grandpa, had been called *El Camino Real*, the King's Highway, the Spanish trail connecting east Texas with Mexico. We crossed the Colorado on a horse-powered ferry and entered the busy little village. I pulled up. "Who are we looking for here, Sister?"

Sister Rossetta's baby face had grown thinner over the last few days. I could see the weariness in her eyes. "A family named Sims, Mr. Burnett. His first name is Jameson. They're from Alabama."

I nodded to Mary Elizabeth. "That her last name?"

The little blond girl answered. "Ballenger, Mr. Burnett. My last name is Ballenger."

"She's never met this part of her family," Sister Rossetta offered.

I surveyed the small town. Several folks along the plank boardwalks stopped to stare at us. At the end of the block was a newspaper office, *The Bastrop Advertiser and County News*. We stopped at the hitching rail, and Sister Rossetta and I went inside.

A wizened old man looked up from a battered desk. A friendly grin split his wrinkled and weathered face, and he rose quickly. "Howdy do, Sister, mister. New to town, huh?"

"Howdy. You the owner?"

He shook his head. "Nope. Just looking after it while he goes home to dinner."

Sister Rossetta stepped forward. "We're looking for a family by the name of Jameson Sims. I understand they live around here."

The friendliness faded from his face, replaced by a deep frown. "He a friend of yours, Sister?"

"I've never met him." She glanced up at me, taken aback by the old man's sudden change in attitude.

He eyed me suspiciously. "What about you, stranger?"

"I'm with her. Wouldn't know the gent if he walked in on me right now."

The old man sneered. "He'd better not if he knows what's good for him. Now I don't know what you folks want with Sims, but if we find him, we'll blame well find hisself stretching hemp from the nearest tree."

Sister Rossetta caught her breath. I cleared my throat. "What's the problem with the Sims hombre?"

"He's a thief. Been living right here in the middle of us for the last four years, all the while stealing us blind and selling the stock down in Smithville. Why, it wasn't more than two weeks ago he was caught redhanded with seven head of stock and each one worn a different brand. He skedaddled out of town just ahead of a necktie party."

I didn't know what to say, so I just left it up to Sister Rossetta. Her voice was level and calm. "Was he married?"

The old man snorted. "Him? Not likely." His eyes narrowed. "You have business with him or something, Sister?"

She shook her head slowly. "No. I must have the name wrong." She looked out the window at Mary Elizabeth. "The man I was looking for would not be a thief."

"Well, then, I reckon old Jameson Sims wasn't the one you was looking for. Whoever gave you his name was either joshing with you or didn't know what he was talking about."

We paused on the porch outside the newspaper office, a frown on both our faces. I glanced at Alicia and the girls, unable to keep from noticing how the sunlight shone on her red hair.

Cautioning the girls to remain in the buckboard, Alicia climbed down and came up to us. She looked from one to the other. "Something wrong?"

I glanced at the girls who were watching her curiously. "Yeah." I kept my voice low. "The hombre we came to see has skipped out ahead of a necktie party."

Alicia's eyes grew wide. She stared at Sister Rossetta, who nodded. "He's right. Mr. Sims is gone." She paused, then added, "None of this makes any sense to me, Mr. Burnett. Why would this Sims person claim he was Mary Elizabeth's kin?"

I could think of two or three explanations, none of them pleasant, and certainly none I would reveal to Sister Rossetta or Alicia. "He mighta been kinfolk, Sister. Even thieves have families." I gave them a crooked grin. "But according to the old gent inside, Sims is gone. So now what about the girls?"

Faster than a bronc can hump his back, Alicia replied, "They can go with me."

We both gaped at her.

She nodded emphatically. "I can look after them when I move in with my aunt. When I save enough money, we can find a place of our own."

Sister Rossetta blinked her eyes. At first, I thought the wind might have blown some dust in them, but when I looked again, I saw tears gathering in the corner of her eyes. She laid her hand on Alicia's arm and squeezed. "The Holy Father St. Matthew will bless you, child."

"And," Alicia added, "the girls can stay with my aunt while we search for the gold."

For several seconds, I stared at the two women who

were looking into each other's eyes. Neither said a word, so I broke the silence.

"Well, ladies, that being the case, I reckon we'd better push out." I glanced at Mary Elizabeth and Carmaline from the corner of my eyes. "What are you going to tell the girls about all this?"

Sister Rossetta looked up. "The truth, Mr. Burnett. That Mary Elizabeth's uncle left town and no one knows where he is."

Alicia added, "And that they are going to live with me."

"But what if they want to know what happened to him?"

A sly smile played over Sister Rossetta's lips. "They won't, Mr. Burnett. They won't."

I arched a skeptical eyebrow, but she was right. Mary Elizabeth nodded her understanding, and both girls clapped their hands and hugged Alicia when the sister informed them of the living arrangement.

Before we left Bastrop, I spent six dollars on food staples, flour and coffee, and a couple cans of peaches for the girls. Just after noon, we pushed out of town, heading for Austin some thirty miles distant.

Mid-afternoon, we paused in a grove of giant pecan trees on the banks of the Colorado, where the river made a large bend. Below, a bed of sand stretched several hundred yards. Sister Rossetta decided that was where we would camp. The sandy bed at the river's edge provided easy access to the river.

"We need to wash our clothes and freshen up for tomorrow," the sister announced, eyeing the children. Obediently, they nodded, and as one, turned their eyes on me.

Well, I didn't need someone to whop me between

the eyes with a singletree. I knew when someone didn't want me around. "Tell you what, Sister. Why don't you ladies go on down and take care of whatever females . . . young ladies do, and I'll run us down some meat for supper and mix up a batch of biscuits and gravy."

Deer were plentiful. Within minutes, I had thick steaks sliced from a haunch and broiling over the fire. Coffee simmered at the edge of the coals, biscuits browned in the makeshift rock oven I constructed, and thin gravy bubbled in the cast-iron spider.

Sister Rossetta and Alicia returned sometime later. Alicia had a scrubbed-new freshness about her. Her eyes danced, and laughter rolled from her throat. "Those girls are having a wonderful time," she said, nodding toward the bluff overlooking the river.

I hesitated. Alicia's eyes twinkled in amusement. "Go ahead. You can look."

Below, Mary Elizabeth and Carmaline frolicked at the river's edge, splashing the green water at each other and screaming at the top of their lungs.

After we ate, the women sat around the fire and sang old songs like "Jeannie with the Light Brown Hair" and then polka-type songs. Then they sang some I'd never heard. One, "Silver Threads Among the Gold," made me remember my family and my days as a youngster in the redlands over in east Texas. The first few years after pa settled us there from out of Tennessee were some of the happiest I recollect. We were so poor—shoe-leather soup was a specialty—but pa and ma were always laughing.

Strange how things happen. Like I said, the sister

and the girls were singing, and I was recollecting, thinking back about the years gone past. When they finished, Sister Rossetta must have spotted the dreamy look on my face, for she asked, "Where do you hail from, Mr. Burnett? Texas?"

Her question caught me by surprise. "Huh? Oh yeah, Sister. Over near Injun Bayou on the Sabine River."

Alicia smiled brightly at me. "Is that where your folks live?"

I thought I'd pushed that hurt behind, but I hadn't. I don't reckon a body can get rid of some things. "They're dead."

The smile on her face vanished. Her brows knit. "I'm sorry, Jack."

With a shrug, I replied. "A long time back. Almost fifteen years."

The camp grew silent. They were all looking at me. I shifted under their gaze. Suddenly, it dawned on me: All of us, maybe even Sister Rossetta, were paddling the same canoe. All of us had lost family.

"Scavengers, the neighbors said." I shook my head. "I don't know. I was twelve. Out hunting, a few miles from home. When I got back, my folks, my grandpa, and my brother had been killed." I hesitated. "Whoever did it, they took everything they could carry."

The frown on Alicia's face deepened. "What did you do?"

"Only thing I could. Stayed on the farm. I was close to being grown-up."

Carmaline spoke up. "But you were only twelve. That's how old I am. Who made your meals?"

I chuckled. "When you live by yourself, young lady, you learn in a hurry."

Sister Rossetta rose, clapped her hands, and said, "That's enough, girls. Time for bed. And don't forget your rosaries." She gave me a smile, and then climbed into her own bed.

The fire burned low, but sleep evaded me. Their questions had dredged up old memories—painful, poignant memories. A new moon rose, a silver crescent, casting a pale light across the flood plains beyond our grove of pecan trees.

In the dark hills far to the east, a coyote howled a plaintive, mournful cry. I stared at the sound, still remembering the east Texas woods.

A few dying embers popped and cracked. I reached for another log and froze. To the east, two shadows on horseback rode across the flood plain, heading north. I glanced at the fire. It was low, and I had built it behind a deadfall of cottonwood. I tossed the log aside and scrabbled into the surrounding darkness so I could keep an eye on the riders.

I watched until they disappeared into the night.

Chances were they were just drifters, but why travel at night unless they had someplace to go? I'd drifted myself. The only time I rode at night was if I was hardpressed for time.

Tomorrow, I had better keep my eyes moving.

Chapter Nine

We pulled out with the sunrise, following the road to Webberville and then on to Austin. I said nothing about the two riders. There was really nothing to say. As far as I knew, they were simply two travelers anxious to reach Austin. Still, I wondered. I couldn't put my finger on what bothered me about them. But something didn't seem right.

Just before dark, we topped a hill and the lights of Austin City flickered in the distance, the yellow glow shimmering in the soft breeze. I felt a pang of regret, and I realized it was because Alicia Wells and I would soon be going our separate ways.

With a click of her tongue and a slap of the reins, Sister Rossetta sent the team down the hill toward the town.

Austin City was a busy, bustling town sitting on a rise overlooking the Colorado River. We rode into town and pulled into the first livery. The hostler pointed us to the Mission de Santiago, where they were happy to put us up for the night. Sister Rossetta and the others went inside while I drove the team into the stable.

I had forty-six dollars in my pocket, but twenty-five of it, half of what I took from the Comanchero, was for the family of McKeever, my dead partner. So naturally I was right pleased not to have to fork over any greenbacks for a night's lodging.

Before I could unhitch the team, Sister Rossetta returned. "Alicia and the girls decided they wanted to go on to Alicia's aunt's house tonight, Mr. Burnett. It isn't far. Will you drive us?"

I hesitated, trying to hide my disappointment that Alicia Wells was leaving so soon. With mixed feelings, I replied, "Sure. Be pleased." But I wasn't. Reluctantly, I put the horses back into the traces.

Alicia and the girls came into the stable, and I helped them into the buckboard. Sister Rossetta and Alicia sat on the seat, scooting over to make room for me.

I picked up the reins. "You know where we're going, Sister?"

She shook her head. "Father O'Toole is accompanying us. He'll be right here."

Sure enough, seconds later, a grinning pixie of a man hurried in and climbed up behind the seat with Carmaline and Mary Elizabeth. "Take a left at the gate, and then turn right at the first corner."

The lamps shining through the windows of the buildings lining the street lit our way faintly. "Two corners up and turn left," the priest said, his voice eager and enthusiastic.

Within minutes, we pulled up in front of a two-story clapboard house with a fresh coat of whitewash. A light shone faintly in an upstairs room. The other windows were dark. I whistled to myself. Alicia and the girls were going to be living in a bed of four-leaf clovers.

Alicia climbed down and turned back to me. "Thank you, Mr. Burnett." I thought I saw a wistful frown flicker over her face. "I know you went out of your way to bring us here. I'll never forget that."

All I could do was nod.

She stood for a moment, looking at me. I knew she was waiting for me to say something, but my tongue was stuck between my teeth.

With a shy smile, she ducked her head and turned back to the house.

Carrying their meager belongings in bundles under their arms, Alicia and the girls, accompanied by Sister Rossetta, climbed the steps and knocked.

Upstairs, a face came to the window, then disappeared, and the light faded, to reappear moments later downstairs. The door opened, and I made out the silhouette of a slender woman, her hair encased in a night bonnet. She extended the lamp in her hand to better see her visitors. The lamplight lit her hatchet face in sharp relief, revealing thin lips drawn in a straight line. Her expression wasn't friendly.

I heard the muttering of words. The expression of disdain on the woman's face remained unchanged. She nodded to Sister Rossetta, then stepped back, admitting Alicia and the girls.

The sister stepped back, and after the door closed she returned to the buckboard.

"That the aunt, Sister?" I clicked my tongue and swung the team back toward the mission.

The everpresent smile had vanished from Sister Rossetta's face. "Yes."

I glanced at her. She sounded none too happy, but I didn't question her. I figured maybe I should keep my mouth shut.

Father O'Toole and his folks were good hosts—hospitable, thoughtful. But I had an empty spot in my chest I couldn't fill. The small, neat room they gave me for the night was too confining, so after everyone had climbed into their bunks, I went outside to the stable.

Just before I reached the stable, I noticed two cowpokes riding past. When they spotted me, they kicked their ponies into a trot. I watched them disappear down the street. With a shrug, I stepped through the stable door.

Fishing around in my gear, I dug out the bottle of Monongalhela Whiskey and threw my soogan on a pile of hay. I flopped on the tarp. For a brief moment, I wondered about the two riders, but quickly dismissed them from my mind.

There were only a couple inches of whiskey left in the bottle, and I made quick work of it. The raw whiskey burned my stomach. For a moment, I considered paying a visit to one of the local saloons down the street, but, considering I had no job and limited funds, figured the smart move was to stay where I was. After deciding to put some distance between myself and Austin City come morning, I drifted off into a restless sleep.

I jerked awake at the jangle of glass against metal. A match flickered. Moments later, the yellow glow from the barn lantern illumined the stable. Sister Rossetta held the lantern over her head, searching the barn for me. In the next instant, Alicia Wells stepped into the light.

"Mr. Burnett," the sister called out.

I sat up. "Over here, Sister."

With Alicia on her heels, Sister Rossetta hurried to me. "Good," she said, smiling broadly. "It's time. Breakfast is ready. I'd like for us to leave before sunrise."

I scrubbed my eyes with my fists. What the blazes was she talking about? I glanced at Alicia who was smiling at me. She was wearing a fresh change of clothes, but her skirt was still one of those split ones, made especially for riding. "Leave? Leave for what?"

Surprised, Sister Rossetta replied. "Why, for Black Mountain and the gold of course. I've made all the arrangements."

I staggered to my feet, brushing the straw from my worn clothes and shaking the sleep from my eyes. "Oh no, Sister. I got you here. That's all I promised. What about Alicia's cousin? I thought he was the one who was going to take you on this wild goose chase."

The young woman's face crinkled into a frown. "He can't help," she whispered, struggling to hold back the tears.

"What?" I looked from her to Sister Rossetta and back again.

Sister Rossetta explained. "Alicia and the girls are back with us."

"What?"

"Alicia and the girls are back with us, Mr. Burnett."

I was still groggy from sleep. All I could say was "What?"

Shaking her head, the sister rolled her eyes. "Heavens, Mr. Burnett. We must work on your vocabulary. Now, quickly, come along. I'll explain over breakfast." Without another word, she turned and, with Alicia on her heels, left the stable, leaving me in the dark—in more ways than one.

I stared after the yellow circle of light crossing over the quadrangle to the main building. On one hand, Sister Rossetta's bland assumption I would do whatever she wanted nettled me. On the other, the fact that Alicia was back gave me a warm, happy feeling.

The dining area was a rectangular room filled with half a dozen fifteen-foot sawbuck tables. A partition separated the dining room from the kitchen. During the summer, the heat was a close second to intolerable, but in wintertime the partition was removed so the heat from the kitchen could warm the dining room.

Father O'Toole sat at the sawbuck table with us while the cook, a little Mexican *señora*, brought us a steaming pot of six-shooter coffee, a platter of hot tortillas, and a plate of sliced beef.

I glanced around, looking for Carmaline and Mary Elizabeth.

"They're still sleeping," said Sister Rossetta. "They will remain here in the mission while we undertake our search."

I gave Sister a puzzled look. Alicia must have spotted it, for she spoke up. "My aunt didn't want the girls."

"That's why they're back," the sister added. "And to make matters worse, Alicia's cousin—you remem-

ber, the young man who was going to take us to Black
Mountain—well, he's gone to California.'' She paused
and stared at me as if everything should be as clear as
spring water.

I stared back. Nothing was clear. In fact, the entire
situation was muddier than those flooded rivers we'd
crossed. Of course, I was happy Alicia was back, but
I knew that there were two sides to everything. A jasper's got to pay to get something good.

I cut my eyes to Alicia, then to Father O'Toole. He
wore a faint smile, as if he knew some big secret. I
nodded. ''So?''

Sister Rossetta shrugged and rolled a tortilla around
a slice of beef. ''So, you can take us to Black Mountain, Mr. Burnett. After all,'' she added before I could
object, ''you've nothing better to do. No place to go.
And just think how much good we can do with the
gold.''

My coffee mug slipped out of my hands and
bounced on the table, spilling the steaming liquid in
my lap. With a shout, I jumped back, brushing frantically at my jeans. I looked up at her, sputtering.

She gave me one of her big smiles and handed me
a towel. ''We truly do need you, Mr. Burnett,'' she
said. ''I've asked Father O'Toole, and he knows of no
one to recommend as our guide.''

My ears burned. I glared at the sister. I drew a deep
breath and blew it out noisily.

Alicia stared at me, her eyes imploring.

I was whipped.

Sister Rossetta was right: I had no plans, no direction, no aim. I just didn't like the idea of her tending
my business, telling me what I was to do or not to do.
That's why I was being so bull-headed, but when I

saw the plea in Alicia's eyes, I caved in. I think I could have stood up to Sister Rossetta. She was tough and determined, but I could be stubborn too. Put those forces against each other, and a jasper might as well count on a Mexican standoff.

Alicia was the one who tipped the scales.

My shoulders sagged. I shook my head. "One of these days, Sister, I'm going to surprise you and do what I want to do."

She smiled and nodded. Her eyes twinkled. "I know, Mr. Burnett, I know."

During breakfast, I listened again as Sister Rossetta read the directions her great-great-great aunt had written concerning the location of the gold.

"In the middle of the Black Mountains is a very rough pass in which there exists a cave of bees. Once through the pass, a horseshoe bend in the Colorado River is plainly seen. On the east side of the bend is a sheer bluff of limestone, facing west. On the south slope of the bluff is a tunnel behind a boulder. The rock with the visage of a demon looks at the gold."

I looked up. "Sounds simple enough."

Sister Rossetta beamed. "You see, we can probably find the gold and return the same day."

Father O'Toole arched an eyebrow.

I snorted. "Don't count on it, Sister. First, we don't even know where Black Mountain is." I turned to the priest. "How about it, Father? You know where it is?"

"No, I've never heard of Black Mountain." He glanced sheepishly at Sister Rossetta. "But I have heard of a cave of bees."

"Nothing unusual about bee caves," I replied,

pouring another cup of coffee and stirring in a goodly amount of sugar.

"I agree. I've never seen this one, but I've been told there are stories from the older settlers about a bee cave deep in a rugged pass within sight of the river."

Alicia's face lit up. "Maybe that's it."

"What do you think, Mr. Burnett?" Sister Rossetta looked up at me earnestly.

I drained the last of my coffee and sat the cup back on the table. "Beats me. I suppose it would be as good a place as any to start."

Sister Rossetta clapped her hands, and Alicia pressed her fingers to her lips. I doused their excitement with cold water. "Odds are ten thousand to one this is the right cave. If we can even find it," I added.

I nodded to Father O'Toole. "We need gear, Father." I eyed Sister Rossetta skeptically. "Even though I think we're chasing the wind, I'm not particularly anxious to fill our warbags in the middle of the day. Someone might get curious. I'd feel a lot more comfortable if you could supply us our needs. I've got twenty-one dollars to buy you some new gear to replace what we take. I got another twenty-five, but I planned on sending that to the family of my partner who the Comancheros murdered."

He shook his head adamantly. "Forget the money, Mr. Burnett. Whatever we have is yours."

Sister Rossetta spoke. "What do you mean, chasing the wind, Mr. Burnett?"

I faced her. "Just what I said, Sister. I don't think there's gold out there, but if someone spots us rigging up for a gold hunt, we'll have company. I guarantee that if you head down the street with a packhorse loaded with shovels and picks, someone will be tagging after. So I don't want anyone to know what we're up to. Understand?''

For once, Sister Rossetta had no opinion. She simply nodded and replied in a soft voice, ''I understand.''

I hesitated, waiting for one of them to ask the question. When they didn't, I decided to keep my plans to myself.

''Something wrong, Jack?'' Alicia frowned at me.

I shrugged. ''Not really. I'm just thinking about the three of us heading out by ourselves. We could run into a heap of trouble.''

Alicia stuck out her jaw. ''Don't forget, Jack, I can use a gun too.''

I chuckled. Why was I worried? The three of us had fought the wilderness for over a hundred fifty miles. I reckoned we could go another hundred fifty if we had to.

Chapter Ten

Next to the stable was a small room stacked with a wide assortment of tools, the usual fare of essential hand implements to maintain a garden for the mission.

I found an ample supply of shovels and picks and axes, which I rolled inside our soogans and lashed to pack saddles. I planned to load our animals during the night and hide them a few miles outside of town. But I kept my plans to myself. The only way for two jaspers to keep a secret is if one is dead.

When the three of us rode out the next morning, I wanted it appear that we were simply taking a leisurely ride around the countryside.

Human nature being what it is, folks would immediately become curious if they spotted a party riding out, leading pack horses burdened with a supply of food and tools.

By mid-afternoon, I had our gear ready. I stashed it in a stall at the rear of the stable, one that could not be seen from the door or windows in the front of the building. All that was left was to lash the packs to the horses.

Now I had to find a secluded spot to hide the ponies.

Saddling the chestnut, I rode out east, on the road to Manor. Luxuriant tallgrass swayed with the breeze sweeping across the rolling countryside. In the valleys, blackjack and post oak mixed with cottonwoods, and pecans lined the drainages.

A few miles out, I cut back north, starting a large semi-circle around Austin City. To the northwest, the hills grew steeper. After passing the Round Rock road, I found a small box canyon with sweet water and abundant graze. A few ropes lashed across the narrow entrance to the canyon, and I had an ideal corral.

Backtracking, I came back into Austin on the Elgin road just before sundown. I kept the details of my plan to myself.

Inside the kitchen that evening, we sat around the supper table going over our plans once again. "Soogans, tarps, lanterns, two weeks' supply of grub. A couple hundred rounds of ammunition for the saddle guns. Both the Comancheros' rifles are .44-40s. I've a couple boxes for my Henry. Three shovels, picks, and a double-bitted axe." I looked at the priest. "You think of anything else, Father?"

"No, Mr. Burnett. I'm no outfitter, but I think you probably have all the gear you need."

I eyed Alicia and Sister Rossetta. I wasn't completely comfortable with the makeup of our little party, but there wasn't a heap I could do about it. But to be honest, even if I could have done something, I don't know that I would have.

"Now, Father, how do we find the bee cave?"

He unfolded a sheet of thick paper and smoothed it on the table. An X on one side indicated Austin City. A line went due west to another X. "That's Oak Hill. Can't miss it. Take Conner's ferry across the river and stay on the road. About ten or twelve miles. Then at Oak Hill, the road makes a Y. Take the right fork. It hasn't been used much the last few years, so I've been told. It leads to the river. About another eight or ten miles." He paused and looked up from the rough sketch. "From what the old man told me, this road out of Oak Hill will take you right through the pass to the river."

I studied the ferry crossing, wondering if there was another ferry upriver where we would actually attempt to cross. I decided against asking. I'd learned years back that the best way to keep a good poker hand secret is to hold it close to your vest.

"Sounds good to me," I replied, letting the three of them believe we would take Conner's ferry across the Colorado.

Alicia spoke up. "Seems simple enough to find, doesn't it?"

"Yep. Almost too simple."

Sister Rossetta frowned. "What do you mean?"

I glanced at Alicia, then turned to the sister. "Hard to explain, but seems like anytime something comes too easy, there's a passel of trouble on its heels."

The three of them frowned. I chuckled and pushed away from the table. "But maybe it's going to be just that simple." I stretched my arms over my head, flexing my fingers and feeling the dull pain in my forearm. It had healed well so far. "Reckon I'll turn in, folks." I had to hide our ponies and get my carcass back before moonrise. I paused at the door and looked back at them. ''We'll pull out just after sunrise.''

Crossing the quadrangle to the stable, I made a pretense of stretching and yawning, putting on a show for anyone who happened to cast a glance in my direction. There were several walkers and riders on the street, which in a busy city like Austin was to be expected.

Inside, I moved both ponies to the rear stall before lighting the lantern and hanging it near the front door. If anyone was curious, I was merely making ready for bed. I spread my soogan on the hay, turned off the lantern, and hurried to the back of the stable.

I cast open a shuttered window, and by starlight rigged the two ponies, after which I saddled my chestnut.

Easing to the front window, I peered over the sills, studying the darkness outside. I could see nothing. I tugged my hat down on my forehead. ''You're wasting time, Jack,'' I whispered, taking the reins of the three horses in hand and leading them through the rear door to the back of the mission.

I paused in the alley behind the church walls. I laid a hand across the muzzle of my chestnut. In the distance, a voice shouted and a dog yelped.

Then, silence.

I swung into the saddle and led the ponies from the alley and out the east road toward Manor. A short piece out of town, I pulled up, ears tuned to the sounds of the night. I could have sworn I heard the nicker of a pony. I listened for several minutes, and all I heard were crickets and the distant howl of a wolf.

Two hours later, I hid the ponies in the box canyon, and backtracked to the Manor Road. Just before I reached Austin City, I cut south so I could come into town on the Webberville road.

The sun rose in a cloudless sky. The wind had switched to the northeast, a fresh breeze that made you want to run through the dewy grass barefoot.

When Sister Rossetta and Alicia entered the stable, they both stopped and looked around, puzzled. Sister Rossetta spoke up. ''Where are the pack horses, Mr. Burnett?''

I lifted an eyebrow. ''Waiting for us, Sister. Waiting for us.''

A knowing smile played over Alicia's lips. Instantly, she sensed what I had done.

We rode out with the sun, heading north toward Round Rock. I carried a straw basket over my saddle horn. To the casual eye, we appeared to be going out for a picnic.

There were a few travelers on the road. We exchanged nods, a couple words, all without stopping. Finally, I cut west off the Round Rock road and pulled up on a small rise a quarter mile distant.

Sister Rossetta frowned. ''Why are we stopping? It's still early.''

I surveyed the country surrounding us. ''Humor me, Sister. I just want to make sure no one else is interested in us.''

Alicia pressed her hand to her mouth. ''You think we're being followed?''

I grinned down at her. ''No, but it won't hurt to be extra careful. You and Sister have a lot at stake.''

Dismounting, I made a show of spreading the blanket. Alicia sat with the basket. I tended the ponies, while Sister Rossetta and Alicia studied the countryside.

"Nothing out there, Mr. Burnett," whispered the sister.

My gaze swept across the rolling hills to the east. Back to the west, the country grew rougher with limestone bluffs and deep, narrow canyons. "Let's give it a few minutes," I replied, suddenly wary but of what. I couldn't guess. With a grimace, I plopped down beside them and reached for the loaf of bread.

The day was one of those rare summer days that made me feel like a boy again despite the nagging at the base of my skull. Clouds drifted across the brittle-blue background, pushed by a gentle wind that constantly changed their puffy white heads from steamboats to birds to giants.

I could almost hear the creek of my youth, smell the rich, earthy soil, and see the same clouds tumbling overhead.

Jerking myself back to the present, I studied the countryside. Quickly, I rose and bundled the blanket. "Let's go."

Moments later, we were twisting down a narrow ravine. At the box canyon, we picked up the pack horses. And then we were on our way again, moving due west. I explained as we rode. "I hid the animals last night. I didn't want anyone to see us leaving with all that gear. We'll come into the bee caves from the north. I don't think we're being followed, but we can't take any chances. Gold makes a jasper do strange things." I kept looking over my shoulder, trying to shrug off the pinprick of uneasiness nagging at me.

Alicia frowned. "I don't understand, Jack. How could anyone know about the gold?"

I nodded toward Austin City. "Father O'Toole knows."

Sister Rossetta gasped. "You can't believe he would say anything."

"No." I grinned at her. "He wouldn't. Not deliberately. But what if someone overheard us talking about it last night? They probably didn't," I added, "but this. . . ." I gestured to the ponies and the surrounding countryside. "This detour is just to put us on the safe side. That's all."

At noon, we reached the Colorado River and broke for a quick meal and short rest. Continuing, I tried to keep us inside the tree line along the riverbank, but there were patches of rolling hills and breaks in the tree line where concealment was impossible.

Mid-afternoon, I pulled up. Ahead the river grew wider. From either bank, a fan-shaped bed of glittering white gravel spread from the shore, meeting in the middle of the river. The sunlight reflected off the green water coursing downstream.

"There's where we cross," I said, sending my chestnut skidding down the steep bank to the gravel. "Follow me, and be careful."

We crossed without incident.

Underbrush and wiry grass choked the slopes, providing us a secure refuge on the west bank. We pulled through the belly high grass and into a copse of new cottonwood. To the west, the sun paused just above the crest of the hills. Below, shadows began filling the river bottom.

I tied the packhorses, then remounted. "I'll take a look around. Get a small fire going. I'll be back directly."

Neither woman argued. They fell to their tasks as I

rode out, first to the south in an effort to cut the bee cave road. An hour later, I pulled up behind a thicket of scrub oak. Overhead, the sky was a sheet of orange and pink, bathing the ground below with reddish hues. At the east end of the valley below, I spotted a small village I figured to be Oak Hill.

With a click of my tongue, I sent the chestnut angling southwest, hoping to cut the road. Ten minutes later, I found it, a narrow trace, overgrown with shrubs and small trees, indicating infrequent usage over the years.

I turned due west, hitting the river a few miles above our camp. There was no moon, and the darkness settling over the countryside forced me to ride in the open to take advantage of the starlight.

Because of the rugged hill country, the Colorado River had more twists and turns than an angry rattler. Even though I knew the limestone bluff marking the gold was farther upriver, I couldn't help searching the dark shorelines below.

Suddenly, I caught a whiff of wood smoke. I reined up and sat silently. Below in the river, the gravel bed we had earlier crossed stood out like a white ghost in the darkness.

I glanced around, searching the darkness out of habit, still trying to shake the feeling that something was out of place. I had heard nothing out of the ordinary, only the usual night sounds. Still, a jasper couldn't be too careful.

Alicia and Sister Rossetta were waiting expectantly when I pulled into the copse of cottonwood. On the edge of the coals, a pot of coffee bubbled, and a batch of stew simmered in the cast-iron spider. The dancing flames cast an orange and yellow glow on the canopy of leaves above our heads.

"Well, all the comforts of home," I said, dismounting, noting the gear had been stripped from pack-horses, and the animals staked and hobbled in good graze.

Alicia smiled warmly. "Stew's about ready."

"Did you find the road, Mr. Burnett?" The firelight flickered across Sister Rossetta's baby face.

"Yep." I nodded southwest. "About an hour or so that way. We should hit it before the dew dries in the morning."

She and Alicia beamed at each other. "It won't be long now," said Sister Rossetta.

With a grunt, I squatted and reached for the coffee. "Well, now, Sister. I don't mean to throw cold water on your hopes, but don't start spending that gold yet."

With a puzzled expression, Sister Rossetta looked at me. "But what do you mean, Mr. Burnett? You know where the bee cave is, don't you? All we have to do is travel through the canyon and there is the limestone bluff."

I sipped the coffee, feeling the warmth flow into my veins. "It just might be that simple, Sister. On the other hand, it might not. I found the road that leads to the cave. We ought to reach the canyon somewhere around mid-afternoon." I glanced at Alicia. "Then we'll know."

We rode out next morning, within the hour intersecting the Bee Cave road. Alicia peered up and down the overgrown trace. "Looks like some time since anyone came this way."

I led the way west along the narrow road. A thick

layer of wiry grass covered the wagon tracks, between which bunches of switchgrass grew. Springy oak limbs drooped in our path. The road curved gently to the northwest. An hour later, we spotted the canyon.

"Is that it?" Sister Rossetta whispered.

Alicia replied softly. "I don't know. What do you think, Mr. Burnett?"

I studied the rocky bluffs, two sheer plates of limestone rising over a hundred feet in the air, looking down on the narrow trail between them.

"Whoa, boy," I muttered, tightening the reins on the chestnut.

"What's wrong?" Sister Rossetta pulled up beside me.

"I don't know." The canyon was just wide enough for two wagons abreast. I shivered. The cramped confines of the narrow canyon made me uneasy. I glanced up at the canyon rim, immediately recognizing that once we entered the close passage, we were easy pickings for anyone above.

Chapter Eleven

The noonday sun beat down on my shoulders. Sweat ran down my spine. I removed my battered hat and dragged my arm across my forehead as I studied the canyon, the limestone walls a brilliant white in the glaring sun. I tried to put my finger on whatever was disturbing me, but it remained just beyond my grasp.

Alicia pulled up beside Sister Rossetta and her eyes followed my gaze across the canyon. "I don't see anything, Jack."

I forced a chuckle. "Just naturally spooky, Miss Alicia. I don't cotton much to tight spots."

Suddenly, the clatter of a falling rock echoed through the silence of the sun-baked day. My chestnut jitter-stepped. I jerked my head up, searching the rim above, but all I saw was a red-tailed hawk gliding across the cloudless blue sky.

For several seconds, I studied the shrub-studded rim. I shook my head. Time to relax. My imagination was getting the best of me, yet I couldn't shake the feeling of impending trouble.

"Well, ladies," I said, nudging the chestnut into the canyon, "no sense in waiting around here. Let's get on through." We were headed west, but if the instructions were correct, the canyon had to swing around. According to Sister Rossetta's waybill, we were to spot a sheer bluff of limestone on the east side of the river.

The air in the canyon lay still and heavy. The heat seemed to percolate from the rocky ground, baking us like a rock oven.

"I wonder where the bee cave is," Alicia remarked. "Do you think there are still bees in it?"

Ahead, the canyon angled to the right. "Hard to say. I imagine every family within miles got their sweeteners from here. Probably ran the bees out."

Around the bend, we pulled up. The canyon had caved in, filling it with rock and debris to a depth of thirty feet. Sister Rossetta frowned at me. "Now what?"

Dismounting, I handed Alicia my reins. "I'll climb to the top and see what the situation is. We might have to go around," I added, gesturing to the canyon rim.

I clambered up the rocky slope, stumbling over loose rocks while wondering what caused so much of the pass to cave in. Before I was halfway up the incline, I knew we'd have a devil of a time getting the ponies up.

I continued to the top. In the distance, I spotted another bend in the canyon, but in between, almost a quarter mile of the narrow gorge had caved in, a jumble of rocks just waiting to snap a leg on the first misstep.

A strange buzzing came from the rocks at my feet. I glanced down just as a batch of bees swarmed out of the rocks less than a yard in front of me.

I leaped back, spinning in mid-air, and hit the rocky ground running and stumbling down the slope, batting at the whirling, swirling cloud surrounding me.

"Back," I yelled at Alicia and Sister Rossetta. "Get back."

Struggling to maintain my balance, I hopped and bounced down the slope in great, lurching leaps, wind-milling my arms and shouting at the top of my lungs.

I hit the canyon floor in full stride, stretching my lanky legs as far as they would stretch, and raced after the retreating ponies.

Those pesky little buzzards chased me fifty yards down the trail. Sister Rossetta and Alicia had pulled up at the mouth of the canyon, but I shot past them and didn't stop running until I put another hundred yards behind me.

They rode up, suppressing their laughter. "Are you all right, Mr. Burnett?" Alicia's eyes danced merrily.

I gasped for breath. "Yeah. Yeah." I touched the growing knot on my jaw and the one on my forehead.

Sister Rossetta handed Alicia her reins and dismounted. She pushed me to a nearby log. "Here, sit. Let me get the stingers out."

She worked quickly, her slender fingers pushing and probing. "There," she finally said, stepping back. "They shouldn't swell too much now."

I don't know what she meant by "too much," but the knots on my forehead and jaw had already swelled to the size of hickory nuts.

Trying not to laugh, Alicia nodded toward the canyon. "We're not going to be able to go through there, huh?"

Sister Rossetta's baby cheeks dimpled in a smile.

With a wry grin, I replied, "Not quite. Those bees made it plain. They don't want anybody in there. Besides, there's about a quarter mile of cave-in that we'd have to lead the horses over. No way they can cross it without one of them breaking a leg."

Turning her eyes to the canyon rim, Sister Rossetta said, "So we go over."

I looked up at Alicia, then nodded to the sister. "We go over, which shouldn't be that much of a chore."

As proud as I am of Texas, I've got to admit that what we call mountains in central Texas are nothing more than large hills. The real mountains are out in west Texas in the Big Bend country. Black Mountain was a large hill, and using deer trails we reached the crest within an hour. Off to our right was the canyon, curving back to the east.

As one, we scanned the east side of the Colorado River, searching for the sheer bluff of limestone. Sister Rossetta looked up at me, puzzled. "Aren't we supposed to be able to see it from here?"

To our right was the canyon, opening almost directly due east onto the riverbank. "If the waybill was right."

She fumbled in her habit and pulled out the directions. Unfolding the worn pages, she read. "In the middle of the Black Mountains is a very rough pass in which there exists a cave of bees." She paused and looked at us.

Alicia nodded. "We found the canyon and the bees."

Sister Rossetta continued. "Once through the pass, a horseshoe bend in the Colorado River is plainly seen."

I pointed about half mile downriver. "There's the horseshoe."

"And," said the sister, turning back to the directions in her hand, "according to my great-great-great aunt's directions, on the east side of the bend is a sheer bluff of limestone. Facing west."

Brushing her long, red hair over her shoulder, Alicia looked up at me in puzzlement, then turned her eyes back toward the river. She exclaimed, "There's no sheer bluff."

At first, her words didn't register on Sister Rossetta, who continued reading. "On the south slope of the bluff is a tunnel behind a boulder. . . ." Her voice trembled slightly as the implication of Alicia's statement hit her. "With the visage . . . of a demon looking at the gold." Sister Rossetta's words slowly faded away when it was realized just what the younger woman was saying.

And Alicia was right.

Instead of a limestone escarpment facing the bend in the river, a slope of boulders, like talus, overgrown with mesquite and juniper, covered the side of the mountain, ending on the sandy shoreline.

I stood in my stirrups, searching up and downstream. The slow-moving river curved through the steep hills, a sandy bed separating the green water from the limestone on each side of the river. I saw no more canyons cutting through Black Mountain. "This has to be the canyon in the directions, Sister," I said.

"But what about the limestone bluff?" Concern twisted Sister Rossetta's baby face.

From the corner of my eyes, a glimmer of movement on our backtrail caught my attention. I scooted around in the saddle and squinted into the valley below. The only motion I spotted was the gentle fluttering of leaves, the swaying of trees. The uneasiness I'd felt earlier came back to nag at me.

"Is that the spot, Mr. Burnett?" Sister Rossetta was insistent.

I surveyed the valley below a moment longer, then turned my attention back to the boulder-strewn slope across the river. "Hard to say, Sister."

"But there's no bluff," Alicia said.

I shrugged and gave her a wry grin. "Nature has her way, Miss Alicia. What are we looking at here, a couple hundred years? Your aunt . . . how many greats? Three? That's a heap of time, enough time for nature to decide to change the complexion of her handiwork."

A frown passed over Sister Rossetta's face. She pointed to the slope of boulders. "You're saying that's where the limestone bluff was?"

I removed my hat and mopped up my forehead with my shirt sleeve. "I'm saying it could be." I gestured behind us. "There's no more canyons back that way— at least not within sight. This one follows the directions Father O'Toole gave us." I eyed the two. "What we need to do is cross the river and explore the south slope of that hill."

By the time we swam our ponies to the far shore, the sun had set behind the rolling hills. We crossed the strip of sand and clambered up a deeply cut watercourse to the base of the mesquite and juniper-covered slope we planned to search the next day.

We were all exhausted. I laid a fire, and while Sister Rossetta and Alicia whipped up some grub, I backtracked to the river, studying the broad strip of sand lining it. The only tracks for a mile up and downriver were ours and those of small animals.

I peered at the darkening hills across the river. I couldn't shake the eerie feeling that something or someone was watching.

The night passed slowly. I awakened at every small sound. Finally, the gray of false dawn pushed back the night. I rose and stirred the banked fire. Moments later, a cheery flame lit the camp.

Later, as we downed our morning grub, we discussed our plan of search. "What do you figure your aunt meant when she said the face of a demon?" I sipped at my steaming coffee and glanced sidelong at Sister Rossetta.

The small nun arched an eyebrow. "I'm not sure, Mr. Burnett."

Alicia blew gently on the tin mug of coffee she cupped in her two hands. "Maybe an image of Lucifer?"

"You mean the Devil? Horns and all that?"

She looked up at me, the firelight reflecting from her dark eyes. "Why not?"

Sister Rossetta replied, "I've wondered myself."

I glanced at the tree-covered hillside above us. "I'd guess the boulder would have to be good size. Doesn't the waybill say it covered the entrance to the tunnel?

And didn't Father Kino lead donkeys down the tunnel?''

The south slope towered over us—some seven or eight hundred feet, I guessed. ''It's at least half-a-mile wide here at the bottom. We've got a heap of ground to cover.''

After breakfast, I rode back down along the river, backtracking over my trail from the night before.

A mile upriver, I jerked the chestnut to a halt. In the sand before me, two sets of hoofprints emerged from the river, crossed the sandy bed, and disappeared up a watercourse cutting deeply through the steep bank.

I unshucked my handgun and peered up the watercourse.

Nothing.

Glancing back down at the tracks, I noticed they were filled with water, which meant some time had elapsed since the riders had passed. Cautiously, I reined the chestnut around and followed their trail up the watercourse.

A second watercourse intersected the first, ending several feet back in an old sinkhole twenty feet across. The sinkhole was about ten feet deep with a bed of sand and a small pool of water on one side.

On the tree-shaded riverbank above, the trail turned upriver, where the riders put their animals in a trot. I studied the trail. Despite early morning shadows cast by the canopy of pecan and cottonwoods over the layer of rotted leaves blanketing the riverbank, the trail was easy to navigate. I followed the sign almost a mile, but the trail never wavered, the animals never broke gait.

Still suspicious, I pulled up. I chided myself for being so spooky, but the nagging feeling refused to go away.

Chapter Twelve

Morning dew glittered on the wild grass and briars as we peered up the south slope of the hill. The incline was covered with large boulders, junipers with drooping limbs sagging to the ground, and wiry mesquite. I handed Alicia and Sister Rossetta each a six-foot staff I'd whittled out of the mesquite. "It's early. Still some dampness in the air, so most snakes will be in their holes."

Alicia jerked her head up. "Snakes?"

I gave her a crooked grin. "Afraid so. We've got to go on foot. The hill's too steep for the ponies. Poke the grass and rocks ahead of you. Stay clear of juniper limbs dragging the ground."

Sister Rossetta nodded to one of the saddleguns leaning in the fork of a mesquite. "Why not just shoot the snakes?"

I arched an eyebrow. "And let everyone else know where we are?"

105

Her chubby cheeks colored. ''Oh!'' She grinned sheepishly. ''I see.''

''You think we were followed?'' Alicia looked over her shoulder in the direction we had come.

I grimaced, remembering the uneasiness that had been nagging at me. At the same time, I couldn't put my finger on whatever was troubling me. Consequently, there was no sense in upsetting them. ''No, we took too many precautions.''

Dividing the slope into thirds, we separated to begin our search. The boulders were so large, the vegetation so thick, that within minutes we lost sight of each other.

We planned to meet back in camp at mid-day unless one of us found the boulder and tunnel first.

The sun rose, drying the dew and heating the rocks. Sweat soaked my shirt. From time to time, the clatter of rocks echoed across the slope.

I ran across boulder after boulder seated firmly in the slope, but none that looked like a demon, none that looked like anything except a boulder. The truth of the matter was, we had no idea the size or demeanor of the boulder. A boulder to Father Kino might be an overgrown rock to me.

At first, finding a cave in the middle of a hillside slope seemed simple enough, but by mid-morning, when I reached the crest of the hill, instead of the cave, I found four rattlesnakes, six horned toads, and a frightened skunk that I gave all the room he wanted.

A single mesquite grew on top of the hill, casting sparse shade. I checked the rocky perimeter around the tree before squatting against the trunk. I removed my hat and let the breeze cool the sweat soaking my clothes.

Minutes later, Sister Rossetta emerged from behind a juniper a few feet below. She pulled up when she spotted me. A look of disappointment covered her face. "Nothing?"

I shook my head. "Not that I saw. No cave. No boulder that looked like a demon. Just rocks and sun."

The hem of her habit was white from the limestone dust and the scapular over her shoulders had green smudges from juniper branches. She sat by me in the shade. Her baby face was red with heat, and perspiration ran down her chubby cheeks. I figured she must be hotter than a Fourth of July picnic wearing that black habit of hers. But I didn't say anything. From what I had heard about nuns, they just about slept in their clothes.

"Maybe Alicia found something." I could hear the frustration in her tone.

"Well, Sister, you got to understand. It's been a couple hundred years. Not that two hundred years is very long in the scheme of nature, but strange things happen." I hooked my thumb toward the tumble of boulders on the west side of the hill. "Maybe the river rose, ate away at the base of the bluff, and the whole thing fell. Who knows?"

She pursed her lips and frowned. "What if this is the wrong hill?"

I chuckled. "It isn't. Not if the waybill is right. Now if we spend a couple more days here and find nothing, then we'll do some more looking."

The crack of a breaking limb and the clacking of rocks caused us to look around. I thought I heard a faint cry, but at that moment a frightened deer burst from behind a juniper and quickly disappeared behind another. We could hear the clatter of hooves on the limestone as the creature raced downhill.''

''Probably Miss Alicia spooked him,'' I said, watching the juniper for her.

But she didn't appear.

We waited a few more minutes, but the only sound was the soft rustling of the wind in the thin leaves over our heads.

I rose and brushed the dust from my worn jeans. ''Maybe we should go down and meet her. She might have found the cave.''

Alicia was nowhere to be found. She had vanished from the hillside just as silently as the night fades into dawn. Sister Rossetta looked up at me with alarm in her eyes. ''Maybe she went back to camp.''

''Maybe.'' I took the sister's elbow and helped her down the slope, but the sinking feeling in my stomach told me we would not find Alicia waiting for us.

Sister Rossetta called out, ''Alicia! Alicia!''

Her only reply was the faint echo of her words bouncing off the distant hills.

The camp was as we had left it.

The alarm in Sister Rossetta's eyes turned to panic.

''Easy, Sister,'' I said. ''Easy.''

''But she didn't answer. Maybe she fell and hit her head.''

''Maybe. You wait here. I'll go back up and look again.''

''No.'' She shook her head sharply. ''I'll look too.''

There was no sense arguing with her. I didn't even try. ''Okay, but let's stay within sight of each other. She might have rolled under the limbs of a large juniper.''

We separated Alicia's third of the hillside into corridors, planning to search up one, move to the next, and search back to the camp.

Twice, we searched up and down, finding nothing. As we started up the third time, I remembered the faint cry and clatter of rocks just before the deer spooked from the juniper. I had assumed the source of the noise had been the deer bleating as it scrambled across the rocky slope.

I flexed the fingers of my right hand. The pain in my forearm had lessened considerably, and I could use my hand without much discomfort. Shucking my six-gun, I nodded to the crest. "Back up the slope. Remember the deer that spooked? I want to take a look up there."

Sister Rossetta looked up at me, puzzled, but she didn't question me. "Let's go," she said.

Fifty feet below the juniper from which the deer sprang, we found Alicia's staff. Sister Rossetta pressed her hand to her lips and gasped.

My heart thudded against my chest. I looked around, half expecting to see her lying unconscious beneath a juniper or mesquite, but she was not in sight.

"M-Mr. Burnett. What do you think . . . ?"

I waved my hand to silence her. I studied the ground, searching for the slightest sign in the jumble of white limestone, bleached even whiter by the sun. Near where her staff lay, a dirt-covered rock the size of my fist leaped out at me. I knelt and touched my finger to the dirt on the stone. It crumbled at my touch. I turned the rock over. The bottom was bleached white.

Something, or someone, had disturbed the rock. I studied the thin soil, noticing a small indentation with several angles. I tried to fit the stone in the impression. It fit perfectly.

The dirt-stained base of the rock was still cool to the touch, meaning it had been exposed to the sun but a short time. Directly to the east, a few more white stones had been disturbed.

Sister Rossetta watched breathlessly as I slowly inched along the trail. Beneath a mesquite, a leaf made up of leaflets in opposite pairs along a slender spine lay on the stones. I pinched the stem between my fingernails. Moisture oozed from the green shoot.

I rose from my crouch and peered to the east, cursing myself for not taking more precautions. Something had been worrying me, but I had ignored it. And now Alicia could be paying the price.

I tipped my hat to the back of my head and wiped the sweat from my forehead. The trail led through the junipers in an easterly direction. I was concentrating so hard on the trail that I forgot about Sister Rossetta.

When she spoke, I jumped. "What has happened. Mr. Burnett?" Quickly, she apologized. "Oh, I'm sorry. I didn't mean to startle you."

With a sheepish grin, I shook my head. "Forget it, Sister. My mind was a thousand miles away."

"So what do you think happened?" She gestured to the ground at my feet. "An animal?"

I arched an eyebrow. "Yeah, a human animal."

"What . . . what do you mean?"

"Someone surprised her. I don't know how he kept her from screaming, unless he knocked her out." I pointed to the trail of overturned rocks. "He took her that way. See the rocks?"

"I see them, but . . . what about them?"

"He, or they, jarred the rocks loose as they left. The rain and sun combined to bleach the top of these stones, but if you look carefully you'll see some of them have dirt on top, which means they were kicked over as Alicia and whoever the other hombre is passed by."

I flexed my fingers on the handle of my six-gun. "Let's go, but stay behind me." Slowly, I followed the trail, losing it once or twice but always spotting another disturbed stone.

We trailed them for almost a quarter mile, and then the trail vanished when we reached a solid plate of limestone four hundred yards wide, a broad slab bare of any vegetation, any growth.

We criss-crossed the slab several times, but the trail had vanished like a puff of frosty breath on a cold morning.

Frustrated, I exploded in a stream of profanity, forgetting all about Sister Rossetta.

She gasped.

I grimaced and clamped my lips shut. "Sorry, Sister. It's just . . . I'm so . . . so blasted . . ."

"I am too, Mr. Burnett. I know it's exasperating, but we've got to keep trying." She looked around the limestone slab on which we stood. The slight breeze moving up the slope fluttered her black habit. Her pudgy face was red from the heat. "Why would someone do such a thing?"

I continued peering into the thick stand of juniper surrounding us. Two or three ideas had popped into my head, but only one, as far-fetched as it might be, made sense. Someone, somehow, had learned about the gold.

Sister Rossetta's eyes grew wide when I told her my suspicion. "But that's impossible."

I took her by the elbow, and we turned back to camp. "Maybe. But I can't think of anything else. Comancheros might have stolen her so they could sell her down in Mexico, but they wouldn't have been so quiet about it." We stumbled down the slope. "I doubt if it's the work of Indians. Most are up at Fort Sill on the reservation now. No, Sister. The gold is the only possible answer. Someone knows, or at least suspects, what we're up to."

She was puffing from the exertion. "I don't know how, Mr. Burnett. You're the only one we've told about it."

I looked down at her. "Remember back when you first told me about the gold? You said something about no one in Indianola wanting to help."

"That's right," she nodded. "What does that have to do with Alicia?"

I just stared at her, at first not believing the little woman's naivete. Then I remembered the old hostler back at the livery in Cuero. Maybe he heard me ask the preacher about someone helping the nuns. Or maybe someone in the saloon figured it out. That could explain the two riders on the trail, and the two in Austin who spooked when I appeared in the courtyard of the mission. And then yesterday, when we reached the crest of Black Mountain, and I thought I saw movement in the valley.

I shook my head. "We've got problems, Sister. Serious problems." I peered around us, but the juniper trees were so thick, I couldn't see more than twenty or thirty feet. "Someone back at Indianola must have spread word about the gold."

She shook her head emphatically. "No, I don't believe it."

"Believe it. Where gold's concerned, anything's possible. The more I think about it, the only logical explanation is that someone is after the gold, and they think Alicia can help them get it." I told her about the riders. "Of course, both instances could be explained away as something else. But when you start putting the pieces together, it adds up to gold fever."

She stared up at me for several seconds, the disbelief on her face obvious.

A gust of wind blew dust in our eyes. "Come on," I said. "Let's get back to our ponies. We can cover a he-, a lot more ground."

When we reached camp, the red-headed cowpoke from Cuero grinned at us. "Howdy, folks. Been waiting for you." Idly, he scratched at his scraggly beard.

Chapter Thirteen

I froze, my hand inches from the butt of my six-gun. I scanned the juniper surrounding us, but Red was the only jasper in sight.

He chuckled and knelt, touching his fingers gingerly to the coffeepot on the edge of the coals. "Don't worry, there ain't no one else around. They're back in the junipers with that little lady of yours."

Sister Rossetta gasped. "Alicia! You haven't hurt her, have you?"

He stood, his grin twisting into a sneer. "Don't worry, Sister. She ain't hurt. And she won't be . . . when you turn over the gold."

Sister's face paled. "How . . . ? how . . . ?"

I spoke up. "We don't have it."

Red's eyes narrowed. He stared at me, then turned his gaze on Sister Rossetta. "He telling me true? You ain't got the gold?" He hesitated, glared at me, then looked back at her. "Remember, lady. You religious people can't tell no lies."

Slowly, she nodded. "Mr. Burnett is right. We do not have the gold."

The owlhoot studied us. Finally, he must have decided we were telling the truth. "You got a map or what?"

Sister Rossetta cut her eyes up at me in alarm. I shook my head. "Give it to him, Sister." I hoped she realized that we knew all the waybill had to say. We were losing nothing by handing it over to Red. Maybe gaining some important time.

The twinkle in her eyes told me she understood. Without a word, she fished it from her habit and handed it to Red.

His fingers fumbled as he unfolded the waybill and frowned at the note. He looked up at us puzzled. "What the blazes is this?"

I forced a chuckle. "That's exactly what I thought, friend."

"I can't read this."

"Me neither." I nodded to Sister Rossetta. "She can translate, but I'll tell you right now, the words on that waybill are over two hundred years old. No telling what kind of changes have come about on this mountain."

Red jabbed the note at the sister. "Read it."

She obliged.

When she finished, Red looked at me, puzzled. I'm not certain just what he was expecting, but obviously, the sparse information confused him just like it did us.

I cleared my throat. "The young woman. You have what you wanted. Now where is the young lady?"

He grabbed the waybill from Sister Rossetta and clutched it above his head in his fist. "Is this all you got, this Mex jabber?"

"Yes." Sister Rossetta nodded.

He looked at her in disbelief. "You mean, you came all the way from Indianola because of this?"

My guess was right. Word had leaked out back in Indianola.

"Yes." She nodded again.

Red looked at me, the doubt in his eyes apparent.

I shrugged. "I tried to talk them out of it, but Sister Rossetta here is a strong persuader. Now what about our friend?"

Indecision flickered across his face. Without taking his eyes off us, he placed his thumb and forefinger in his lips and whistled. "I ain't fooling around, cowboy. I'll put a hole in your carcass just as fast as I did one of them blasted Comancheros I caught trying to steal a horse back in Cuero."

A wry grin ticked up one side of my lips. "I'd wondered about that one. I took care of his partner upriver."

Red sneered. "Just so you know I mean business."

"I know." I nodded. "I know."

Moments later, two surly cowpokes, one pushing Alicia ahead of him and the other leading their ponies, emerged from the junipers.

"Sister!" Alicia ran to Sister Rossetta and the two hugged.

I remained motionless, not wanting to give the owlhoots a reason to start throwing lead biscuits. "You all right, Miss Alicia?" I kept my eyes on Red and his compadres.

"Yes." She nodded. "They didn't hurt me."

The hardcase leading the horses, a young man with hollow cheeks and greasy black hair to his shoulders, nodded at the sheet of paper in Red's hand. "You got the map there, huh?'' The two cowpokes crowded around their partner.

He handed it to them. ''Such as it is,'' he replied in disgust.

Greasy Hair turned the paper upside down, then right side up. ''What do it say, Red? You know we can't read.''

Eyeing us suspiciously, Red growled, ''It's written in Mexican. Says the gold is right up there, on that hill, and the cave is behind a boulder that looks at the gold. The boulder looks like a demon.''

The other cowpoke, an older man with gray hair, grunted. ''What kinda demon?''

All three looked at us. I shrugged. ''Your guess is as good as ours, partners. We haven't seen anything you could call a demon. Fact is, we haven't seen anything you could call a boulder.''

Red frowned and scratched his head. ''Well, now. I ain't rightly sure just what I'm going to do now.''

I didn't like the sound of that remark. ''Look. You old boys got the directions, such as they are. You can tell from looking at us, we don't have the gold. You keep the waybill. Look for gold. Just let us go.''

He eyed me suspiciously. His two compadres looked at him expectantly. ''I don't know. How do we know you ain't going to get the law after us if we turn you loose. Maybe, we just ought to shoot you dead right now.''

Alicia and Sister Rossetta caught their breath. I chided Red. ''Now you know better than that. You might shoot me, but two women?'' I turned to his partners. ''You boys don't want to kill two women, one a nun, do you? You'd never get another night's sleep.''

Greasy Hair shook his head emphatically. "No, sir. Not me. Not me, Red. We can't kill no women."

The older man agreed.

Red's face darkened. "Then suppose you tell me what we're supposed to do with them, huh? Can't let 'em run loose while we look for the gold."

The three hardcases pondered the problem for a moment, then a grin split the older man's face. "Tie 'em up and keep 'em here with us 'til we find it. Then we can turn them loose."

"Hey, yeah. That's a dandy idea, Red," said Greasy Hair, bubbling with excitement. "We can just tie 'em up and keep 'em here with us."

Alicia and Sister Rossetta looked up at me in alarm. I gave a brief, almost imperceptible shake of my head. Alicia caught it and smiled.

Greasy Hair trussed me up, but Red stopped him from tying the ladies.

"Until tonight," said Red, "you ladies ain't going nowhere without your friend here, so no sense in tying you up right now. But tonight is different. You ain't going to get the chance to hightail it out of here while we sleep."

The older jasper stayed with us that afternoon while Red and Greasy Hair searched the slope. He warned us. "You women try to untie that jasper of yours, I'll tie you both to a mesquite."

The sun baked the limestone. The air was as still as death, for the thick stands of junipers blocked the afternoon currents rising to the crest of the hill. We were sitting in the shade of a juniper. Under her breath, Sister Rossetta whispered, "What are we going to do now, Mr. Burnett?"

I glanced sidelong at Alicia. "You still have your boot gun?"

Under her breath, she replied, "Yes."

"Extra cartridges?"

"A few."

"Let me have them. Drop 'em in my vest pocket."

Sister Rossetta muttered as Alicia furtively did as I asked. "Do you have something in mind, Mr. Burnett?

"Just wait. I've got an idea."

Their faces lit up. Chances are, if they knew what I had in mind, they wouldn't have been so happy. It was a gamble, a wild chance, but it was the only one I could come up with.

When Red and his partners hogtied me, they took my six-gun. The only weapon we had between us was Alicia's little derringer—not the most powerful handgun around, but it was all we had.

Greasy Hair had done a poor job of tying me. I'd kept some slack, which I now worked to stretch. The ropes cut into my wrists, but slowly I gained an extra inch or so. I didn't plan on making a move until after dark. Then, if somehow we could get a couple of the hardcases out of camp, I could slip the ropes and make my move.

Red and Greasy Hair returned just before dusk. He put Sister Rossetta and Alicia to rustling up the grub, sent Greasy Hair to tend the horses, and the old man to bring in more firewood.

Now was my chance.

Keeping my eyes on Red's back, I slipped the ropes from my wrists and retrieved the derringer cartridges from my vest.

Alicia and Sister Rossetta saw me. They hesitated. I shook my head and felt the ground behind me. I seized a good-sized rock. One good blow on the head would put him out. Then we'd have the camp—saddleguns and all.

Just as I started to rise, I heard the clatter of rocks from the direction of the horses. Greasy Hair!

Cursing to myself, I rose to a crouch.

At that moment, Red turned.

Alicia gasped.

Red and I stared at each other a second. "Run," I shouted to the women, while hurling the rock with one hand at the gunman and tossing the cartridges into the campfire with the other.

Off balance, Red stumbled back, but the rock caught him on the forehead, knocking him to the ground. At that moment, Greasy Hair stepped into the clearing. He froze. I scooped up another rock and slung it at him.

He shouted and leaped aside as I hurtled over Red and dashed into the junipers after Alicia and the sister.

The campfire exploded, sending slugs whining in every direction.

"Duck," Greasy Hair shouted.

We dodged through the junipers. Shots broke the darkness, whipping past us. I grabbed Sister Rossetta's hand and raced up the slope, not sure just what I was searching for.

Behind us, the camp was a mass of confusion.

We had to hide and hope the darkness would protect us until we could slip away.

I brushed around a large juniper, its limbs sprawling on the ground. A boulder bulged from the ground in front of the tree. "Here. Under here," I told them in an urgent whisper. "We'll hide under here."

Neither argued.

We crawled behind the boulder and beneath the

limbs. To my surprise, the juniper was growing in a shallow basin no more than five or six feet wide. We had to lie on our stomachs, but the limbs covered us, and with the shadows of darkness we should go unseen. I took Alicia's derringer. If a face did start poking inside the tree, he'd be looking at the last sight he would ever see on this earth.

The shouts started up the slope.

I jammed the derringer back in Alicia's hand. "Here, take it. I've got an idea." Quickly, I slipped from under the juniper and grabbed a small rock. With all my strength, I heaved it as far as I could with my left hand. To my disgust, it hit about fifty feet east of us.

"There they are! Over there!"

With a muffled curse, I winced as I grabbed a rock with my right hand, but I was desperate. I had to take a chance on reinjuring my forearm. Clenching my teeth against the pain, I hurled the rock as far as I could. From the sound of it, the rock struck a couple hundred feet down the slope.

The voices shouted again. "Back east! Over there!"

With a grin, I knew I had thrown them off our trail, at least for the time being. Now should we try to escape up hill or wait? I hesitated, listening to the pursuit heading away from us.

I glanced at the shadows above us. We had no choice. We couldn't take a chance on waiting them out. While there was no moon for a few hours, the starlight reflecting off the white limestone would be just as revealing. Sooner or later, Red and his partners would search the entire slope. We couldn't hide in the shadows of the juniper all night.

Quickly, I skirted the juniper and slipped in from

the back. I slid down in the shallow basin. "Well, I'm . . ." Without warning, the ground beneath me gave way, sending me tumbling backward into a black hole. "What the . . ." A pile of rocks and dust poured over me.

I coughed and choked. I threw out my arms, slapping my hands against rocky walls.

Alicia cried out in alarm. "Jack!"

Chapter Fourteen

I froze. My first thought was I had fallen into a rattlesnake den. I crunched my eyes shut. Every muscle in my body stiffened as I anticipated the first burning strike. My heart thudded against my chest, and I held my breath. Dust settled, clogging my nostrils. I waited, but the strike never came.

Then I heard Alicia's frightened whisper from above. "Jack. Jack. Are you all right?"

I opened my eyes and peered in the direction of her voice. I saw nothing. Cool air from below wrapped around me.

"Are you all right?" Her voice cracked. "You hear me? Are you all right?" Behind her, Sister Rossetta's words stumbled over each other like a herd of steers tearing through a fence.

"Yeah," I whispered. "Both of you be quiet," I said. "I don't know what I fell into here. I sure don't want to spook anything."

She caught her breath, but they grew silent.

Slowly, I reached into my vest pocket and pulled out a match. I hoped the light couldn't be seen from outside. I hoped even more the sudden glare wouldn't spook anything inside.

The match flared. I shot a hasty glance over either shoulder, trying to spot anything behind me. I sighed in relief. Just rocks.

Carefully, I scooted around so I could peer into the darkness below me. From the dim starlight filtering through the juniper limbs, I saw that I was sitting on a slope of rocks that led farther down into a dark hole a couple of feet in diameter. A flame of excitement coursed through my veins. In the next instant, a cold fear chilled my blood.

Often I had heard of the old dried-up artesian wells dotting the chalk limestone in this part of the state, wells that once carried pure and sweet water to the surface from aquifers several hundred feet into the bowels of the earth.

I tried scooting back up the slope, but the rocks slid, carrying me a few more inches toward the hole. I froze, not daring to move. I whispered urgently over my shoulder. "Hand me some kind of rope or something." Sweat popped out on my forehead. I tried to be patient, not to move, not to disturb the unsteady slope of rocks on which I sat, but visions of plummeting hundreds of feet down into a darkened chimney hammered at my patience.

A cloth of some sort fell across my shoulder. Frantically, I grabbed at it with my good hand. I fought the urge to scramble out of the hole before I knew exactly into what I had fallen. I tightened my grip on the cloth, realizing it was the cincture with which Sister Rossetta snugged her habit around her waist.

Pulling a match from my vest, I struck it. The dim glow pushed back the darkness only a few inches. While still holding the match, I picked up a rock with the same hand and tossed it down the hole, expecting long seconds of silence before it struck bottom.

To my surprise, it clattered against more rock almost instantly. An unlikely thought flashed through my head. Trembling with excitement, I tossed another. Again, it hit bottom faster than I could take a breath. ''What about those hardcases? You hear them?''

Sister Rossetta mumbled something to Alicia, who lowered her head into the hole. ''The sister said their voices disappeared down the slope.''

''Good. Now hand me a dead limb,'' I whispered. ''There should be some under the tree. But be quiet.''

I fumbled for another match and lit dried needles on the small limb Alicia passed down to me. Leaning forward, I lobbed it down the hole. The limb flared, revealing what appeared to be a rocky plate extending back into the hillside.

Could it be? My excitement built. ''More limbs,'' I hissed.

''What's down there?'' Alicia whispered as she handed me several more dead branches.

''I'm not sure.'' Releasing my grip on the sash, I fashioned the branches into a makeshift torch. I struck a match to it and dropped it down the opening.

''Well, I'll be ...'' I muttered, seeing what appeared to be a smooth surface a few feet below me. I looked up at Alicia, the dim torch below casting her face in faint shadows. ''Hand me a few more branches if you can find some. I'm going down. Maybe we've found our hiding spot.'' I didn't want to say more, but in the back of my mind, I wondered if we hadn't found the cave of Father Kino.

I grabbed the branches she handed me and slid down the slope of rocks to the flickering torch below, hoping what I had seen was not simply a ledge overlooking an artesian chimney.

At the bottom of the slope, I found myself in the middle of a tunnel, only a few feet wide and less than six high. I laid the branches on the torch, and a small fire lit the cave. I glanced around the rocky floor for snakes, then called out softly to Alicia. "Come on down. There's no danger."

I stood at the base of the rock slide, helping them. The small fire flickered dimly, but provided enough light for us to see that the cave we were in, though small, was large enough for burros. I blinked against the smoke stinging my eyes and motioned Alicia and Sister Rossetta to sit on the backside of the fire to stay out of the smoke being pulled out the mouth of the cave. "We're safe down here. But we can't keep the fire going. They might smell the smoke and trace it to us. I'm going back out to see what those skulkers are up to now. Once I get out, you best put out the fire."

I removed my spurs and turned to leave, but Sister Rossetta stopped me. "Mr. Burnett?"

"Yeah, Sister?" I looked over my shoulder.

She gestured to the tunnel. "Is this it? Is this Father Kino's cave?"

I looked at Alicia, then back at Sister Rossetta. I couldn't resist a grin. "It just might be, Sister. It just might be."

"But the boulder? The one that was supposed to look like some kind of demon . . . where is it?" A frown contorted Sister Rossetta's face.

"You noticed the tree is in a depression. Chances are a landslide or mud slide covered up both the cave opening and the boulder. And the tree started growing. Whatever destroyed that limestone bluff out there could have covered the cave. Now I'll be back. You're safe in here."

Back up on the slope, I lay under the juniper, peering into the night, my ears tuned for any indication of Red or his partners. From down below, voices drifted upward, a mumbling of sounds too distant to understand.

I eased down toward the camp. The three hardcases were squatting around the fire, passing a bottle of Monongalhela Whiskey back and forth. Occasionally, one of their ponies whinnied, but Red and his partners were too busy chugging down whiskey to worry about them.

Within an hour, they had polished off the bottle. Red staggered to his feet and hurled it down toward the river. He turned back to the fire and grinned after it smashed on the rocks. "We'll find them three tomorrow," he declared, swaying on his feet. "Just you wait and see."

The old man spoke up, his words slurred. "You really figure there be a cave of gold around here, Red?"

Red patted his shirt pocket. "This here waybill says so."

Greasy Hair snorted. "The way my luck goes, we won't find nothing."

"Then why don't you mount up and ride on out?" said Red, gesturing toward Austin City.

Greasy Hair shrugged.

Red grunted. He removed his gunbelt and draped it

over his saddle. He tugged off his boots and crawled between his blankets. "If you ain't going to ride out, then you keep first watch."

Minutes later, Red and the old man were sleeping. Greasy Hair did as Red said and took his watch, but within moments after his partners fell asleep, he started snoring too.

At first, I planned to get off the mountain quickly when they fell asleep, but the more I thought about the matter as I watched the three owlhoots snoozing off the whiskey, the angrier I got. I never liked being pushed around or forced to leave someplace against my will. I sure didn't cotton to the idea of being run off while someone stole that which was mine. If I ended up on the little end of the horn because of my own foolishness, I couldn't complain. But to be stuck out there by three drunken owlhoots was just too much for me to tolerate.

I lay behind the juniper watching the camp, trying to figure out how to turn the tables on the three of those hombres. Suddenly, I knew what I was going to do.

I would simply steal our gear back and then proceed to steal all theirs. I would leave them with nothing except a fire and their blankets. I suppressed a chuckle. The way the three were sawing logs, I could probably stampede their ponies through the middle of the camp without disturbing nary a one.

Within the next thirty minutes, I carried off five saddleguns, six canteens, two bags of grub, four saddlebags containing grub, cartridges, and some of Greasy Hair's dirty laundry. I skipped over the saddles, figuring they were too heavy for three jaspers like Red and his boys to attempt to carry back to Austin City.

Once or twice, Greasy Hair stirred, but each time, he squirmed down into a more comfortable slump and continued snoring.

On impulse, I grabbed the old man and Red's boots, which I hid in some nearby junipers. I would have hidden them farther away, but the smell seeping out of those boots was rank enough to gag a dog on a gut wagon.

After depositing the last of the gear in the cave, I handed Alicia a couple saddleguns—rimfire Winchester 66's. "All that's left at the camp are the horses. You wait outside the cave here. When you hear me yell, empty both them guns toward the camp. Hold 'em high. Hate to kill anyone."

"What about you?" The concern on her face was etched in sharp relief by the starlight. "What if I hit you?"

"Don't worry about me. I'll be long gone. Soon as you empty them, slip inside the cave. When I get back, I'll call out before I stick my head down there."

I knelt in the shadows of a juniper near the camp and surveyed the clearing. The three were still snoring. Were they in for a surprise.

Quickly, I untied the ponies. As silently as possible, I moved our three back east. Their hooves clattered and scraped on the rocks. From time to time, one whinnied, and in each instance I expected shouts from the camp.

Finally, I guessed I was far enough. I tied our ponies tight and then hobbled them. I didn't want the commotion to stampede them. I gathered their reins and pulled their muzzles together so I could control them when the shooting began.

If I guessed right, their ponies would head for the river, and when the owlhoots gave chase, I would take ours over the crest of the hill until morning.

Turning my head toward the cave, I shouted, "Now!"

My voice echoed across the slope. There was no response. Had something gone wrong?

Abruptly, the night exploded with gunfire. Slug after slug ripped downhill. Shouts erupted from the camp; horses squealed.

Our own ponies tried to rear and pull away. Cursing, I held them tight, thankful for the hobbles.

Seconds later, the shooting was over.

Across the slope echoed shouts. "Get the horses!"

"No! Down there! The river!"

"Stupid!"

I laughed softly as the trail of curses and shouts drifted down the hill toward the river. By now, our horses were calm. Quickly, I tied them to a strong tree trunk and hurried back to the owlhoots' camp, where I tossed all their belongings, except the coffeepot, on the fire.

Chuckling, I returned to our ponies and led them over the crest of the hill and picketed them in some nice graze. I replaced the hobbles and sat down to wait for morning.

Sometime later, Red's voice echoed up the hill. He tried to sound belligerent, but all he did was whine. "I know you're out there, cowboy, but it just ain't Christian to go stealing nobody's boots with all these rocks around, you hear?"

"Yeah." Another voice joined in. The old man's I figured.

"We're going to find you, and when we do, why . . ."

I shouted down the slope. "I don't figure you to be a smart hombre, Red, but if you got the brains of a horned toad, you and your compadres will hitch up your pants and skedaddle. I got the firepower now, and even if I'm with a nun, I'll put a hole in the carcass of the first one of you three I spot. You hear me?"

A muttering of voices drifted up the slope.

"You mean to make us walk back to Austin City?" Red was almost pleading now.

"Nope. You old boys can swim the river and hike over to Oak Hill. Maybe you can get a ride there." I paused. "Just don't come skulking up here. I ain't blowing no smoke when I tell you I'll stick a lead plug in your hide if I spot you."

Slowly, the muttering faded away. I listened as hard as I could, trying to pick up the scrape of a boot, the rattle of a stone, the brush of a juniper limb. But all I heard the rest of the night was the normal sounds of the darkness.

Once, I thought I heard voices down at the river, but I couldn't be sure. I leaned back against the lone mesquite and stared into the night, wishing I could be sure the three were heading back to Austin.

But I reminded myself: The only way I could be sure they wouldn't try something else was to kill them. And I didn't want to go that far unless there was no choice.

Chapter Fifteen

Before sunrise, I led the horses down the north side of the mountain to the sinkhole I had discovered a couple days earlier. The small enclosure would make an ideal corral for the horses. I wedged broken limbs across the opening and dropped a couple armfuls of grass inside. With the small pool of sweet water along one wall, I figured this ought to keep the ponies fat and sassy. I knew the water was seepage from the river, but I never gave it a second thought. I didn't even notice that the pool was larger than when I first saw it.

I hesitated after climbing out of the watercourse. I looked up and down the riverbank. The early morning sun had yet to penetrate the canopy of leaves overhead. I crossed my fingers. If Red and his boys came back, I hoped they wouldn't swing this far north.

Alicia and Sister Rossetta were waiting for me inside the tunnel.

Sister Rossetta looked up at me anxiously. "Are they gone?"

"Yeah. At least, I think so. I hid the horses back north, so we ought to be in good shape." I nodded toward the darkness of the tunnel beyond. "You looked around?"

"Not far, Jack," said Alicia. "Only to the first bend about fifty feet down there."

"Well then. I reckon we need to see what's beyond."

Sister Rossetta gestured to the floor. "Sit first. Eat something. We didn't make any coffee for fear those outlaws might smell it." She handed me a couple tortillas and some jerky.

"Thanks." I leaned against the wall and tore off a chunk of dried beef. Jerky won't put any fat on a body, but by the time a jasper gets it chewed and swallowed, he's either full or tired of chewing. It took me about ten minutes to put away that hand-sized slab of jerky and wash it down with sweet water.

I was exhausted, but the excitement of what might lie in the depths of the cave charged me with anticipation. Wiping the back of my hand across my lips, I picked up a lantern and lit it. "Well, ladies, let's see what's back there."

The cave was narrow and low. If I extended my arms, I could touch both walls. The ceiling was low enough that I couldn't stand up straight. Closed spaces didn't bother me too much, but I think I would have probably been screaming to get out if I had been in Father Kino's shoes leading fifteen burros through such confines.

One fragment of the story puzzled me, however.

Father Kino led fifteen burros inside, but he returned with none. Had he killed them all? That seemed unlikely. Could they have fallen into a shaft? If so, why hadn't Father Kino mentioned such an incident?

The acrid stench of the coal-oil lantern stung my eyes. Alicia coughed. ''You ladies doing all right back there?''

Sister Rossetta replied in her typical lilting voice. ''As well as can be expected, Mr. Burnett. The smoke is terrible.''

Alicia coughed again.

The cave had so many twists and turns, I had trouble figuring out where we were under the mountain. One thing I noticed, it kept going down.

Abruptly, the cave split, one tunnel turning off at a sharp angle. ''Let's try this one,'' I said, holding the lantern into the offshoot.

Less than fifty feet within, that branch of the cave ended in a jumble of boulders that had caved in. We backed out and continued down the main shaft, expecting to see a room of some sort with stacks of gold or piles of bones.

Thirty minutes later, we rounded a bend and jerked to a halt. In surprise, I looked at my feet. The rocky floor of the cave ended. Ahead, the floor was sand— river sand. The roof of the cave angled downward, disappearing in the sandy floor less than ten feet in front of us.

''Look,'' Alicia said, pointing at the water seeping from the sandy bed.

''We must be near the river,'' I surmised, trying to position us in proximity to the mountain. The truth was, the cave was so twisted and crooked that I had lost all sense of direction. Now I'm no Richard J. Gatlin, but it didn't take someone as smart as the inventor of the Gatlin gun to figure out that a sandy floor with water oozing from it indicated we were near the river.

"But," asked Sister Rossetta in a puzzled voice, "where's the gold?"

I held the lantern to light our faces. "If this is the right cave, the only place it can be is behind the rocks in that offshoot back behind us. There's no other place."

We paused in the second shaft and studied the tumble of boulders sealing the tunnel. By now, not only did our eyes burn from the harsh coal-oil fumes, but we were near exhaustion, having clambered down to the river bed and back up.

"Let's get some fresh air and relax," I suggested. "Then we can come back down."

The journey back up the cave seemed to take forever.

Outside, we moved away from the cave opening beneath the juniper and built a small fire in a small clearing in the midst of the junipers. While Alicia and Sister Rossetta whipped up some noon grub, I wandered the slope, Winchester in hand, looking for some sign of Red and his boys. Once, I heard a clatter of rocks. I ducked behind the thick, green limbs of a nearby juniper and waited. Moments later, a young doe grazed past. I remained motionless. She never spotted me.

While waiting for dinner, I studied over what we had learned down in the cave. Strange how it ended down at the river. Obviously, the cave had once opened onto the shore, but rising water had filled it with sand.

Who could say? Perhaps a slide downriver raised the elevation of the water, submerging the opening, eventually filling it with sand. For whatever reason, Mother Nature has a way of taking care of her own, moving the earth around to suit her needs. She's one lady I wouldn't try to bluff at the poker table. I rubbed my eyes. They burned from lack of sleep.

After dinner, the women slipped back into the cave while I looked around the slope one more time, heading back to the juniper in a roundabout course.

Once back in the cave, I led the way back to the blocked shaft. Sister Rossetta held the lantern, while I struggled to pull boulders from the cave-in.

We worked all afternoon, depositing the boulders along the side of the narrow tunnel. Breathing hard, I pulled a boulder from the top of the pile and stiffened. "I don't believe it," I muttered.

"You find it?" Sister Rossetta's voice trembled with excitement.

Alicia crowded up behind me. "Let's see it! Let's see it!"

I grabbed another boulder and pulled it down, letting it bounce down the slope of rocks. I groaned. Behind the boulders was a solid wall of rock.

"What is it?" A tone of apprehension edged Sister Rossetta's voice.

Staring at the wall, I shook my head. "Nothing." I turned to face them.

"Nothing?" Alicia frowned at me.

"Nothing. A solid wall of rock. That's all it is."

I moved aside so Alicia and Sister Rossetta could see for themselves.

"I don't understand," the sister said, turning from the rocks and staring at me in confusion.

"W-where did all these boulders come from, then?" Alicia wiped her damp hair from her forehead.

"Who knows?" I shrugged. "Cave-in. Maybe someone started digging and found the ground unstable. Maybe it was nothing more than a place to deposit boulders from the main shaft. Could be any of a hundred explanations."

A hurt frown replaced the confusion on Sister Rossetta's face. "Then what happened to the gold?"

I nodded toward the cave entrance. "Let's go on back. We'll try to figure out what our next step is."

She nodded. "Fine, but what about the gold?"

They plodded ahead of me, Alicia in the lead, carrying the lantern. Sister Rossetta had posed a puzzling question. What did happen to the gold? "Two or three possibilities, Sister," I said. "First, wrong cave. Second, someone already has the gold. Third. . . ." I hesitated. "I don't what a third could be. The way I figure is that if this is the right cave, then someone found the gold long ago. The problem with that notion is we saw no evidence of dead animals. Someone comes along and finds the gold, that's what they take. They don't sweep out all the donkey carcasses. There was no sign at all that burros were left in here."

"But this cave has a boulder in front. On the other side of the tree." Alicia spoke over her shoulder.

"All we saw was the top of the boulder. Maybe that isn't a boulder."

Sister Rossetta stopped so abruptly I almost ran into her. She looked at me. "Then, Mr. Burnett, we need to find out if this is the correct cave. We will dig away the dirt and see just what the boulder does look like."

* * *

I knew better than to argue with the sister. While Alicia put a supper together, Sister Rossetta and me got busy on the boulder. I used a grubbing hoe to dig out chunks of rocky soil while she scraped at the loose stuff with a shovel. Since we were working on a slope, the excavation went rapidly.

The boulder was not a large one, perhaps four feet in diameter. Since several inches of the crown were uncovered, we managed to expose almost half of the boulder within half an hour. To our surprise, the boulder was smooth.

If there was a visage of a demon it must have been a plain one, for there was not one marking on the stone that by any stretch of the imagination a jasper could call a feature.

The sun had set earlier, and dusk was shadowing our faces, but the disappointment in Sister Rossetta's face was evident. "This must be the wrong cave."

I leaned on the hoe and peered into the encroaching darkness. "Could be, Sister. Could be," I replied thoughtfully. I glanced at the partially uncovered boulder, then stared in the direction of the river, remembering the steep slope of boulders on the west side of Black Mountain.

Reaching for her shovel, I said, "Let's get our grub and take it back to the cave. We can talk more about it down there."

I paused outside the cave, peering at the black chasm above the Colorado River. A thin fog had formed between the hills lining the river. From where I stood looking down, it appeared like a vaporous white snake twisting through the darkness. I frowned down at the cave opening. For some strange reason, I had the feeling we had indeed found the cave in which Father Kino led the burros.

But there was nowhere inside the cave he could have left the animals. So what the blazes happened?

Alicia gave me a puzzled look when I aired my idea about the cave being the right one. "But where could Father Kino have hidden the gold, Jack?"

We squatted on the cave floor, the lantern between us and the mouth of the cave. The opening drafted the fumes from the oil-burning lamp. I nodded to Sister Rossetta. "Do you remember just exactly what it was that your aunt wrote on the waybill? Maybe we're missing something."

Sister Rossetta arched a skeptical eyebrow. "I remember, Mr. Burnett. I read the note so often that it is committed to my memory." Clearing her throat, she said, "In the middle of the Black Mountains is a very rough pass in which there exists a cave of bees. Once through the pass, a horseshoe bend in the Colorado River is plainly seen. On the east side of the bend is a sheer bluff of limestone, facing west. On the south slope of the bluff is a tunnel behind a boulder. The rock with the visage of a demon looks at the gold."

Alicia spoke up. "But didn't you say the boulder outside the tunnel was smooth? There was nothing about it that looked like a demon . . . or anything."

I nodded yes. But I had the disturbing feeling I was missing something. There was an idea, a thought right on the edge of my consciousness, but each time I reached out for it, it slipped away, back into the darkness.

Sister Rossetta broke into my thoughts. "I think we

found the wrong cave, Mr. Burnett. Tomorrow, we need to start our search once again.''

I wondered. ''Okay, but listen just a minute, Sister. We found the cave of bees and the pass. There weren't any more passes in Black Mountain. We looked.'' I paused.

They both nodded.

''And,'' I said, ''we found the horseshoe bend and the bluff of limestone, except it had caved in. When it did, the bluff left a slope of boulders all the way to the river's edge. And the slope does face west.''

I hesitated, studying Sister Rossetta. ''What were the last couple lines again, Sister?''

She frowned as she replied, failing to understand the point I was trying to make. ''On the south slope of the bluff is a tunnel behind a boulder. The rock with the visage of a demon looks at the gold.''

''We found the tunnel behind the boulder, didn't we?''

Alicia shook her head. ''But it was not the one the demon looked at.''

I nodded. ''My point exactly. Now think carefully, Sister. Did the waybill say the demon looked at the tunnel or at the gold?''

Their frowns deepened. Abruptly, Alicia's eyes grew wide. ''No, it says the demon looked at the gold.''

Sister Rossetta frowned, clearly puzzled.

''Look, Sister, what if this rock is not the boulder with the face of a demon? But this could still be the tunnel.''

And then the idea that had been evading me suddenly exploded in my head. ''If I remember your story, Father Kino led the burros into the caves and remained inside for a long time.''

''Yes.'' Sister Rossetta's frown deepened. ''A very long time.''

''Remember down at the end of the cave?'' I looked at Alicia, who nodded.

''Yes,'' she replied. ''The roof ran into the sand.''

''And,'' I added, ''water seeped up from the sand.'' I continued, growing excited as my little guessing game picked up steam. ''Suppose Father Kino led the burros inside, expecting to find a hiding place and he found exactly what we found—nothing—except down at the bottom the cave opened onto the shore of the river. And it was down there he hid the gold.''

''You mean,'' began Alicia, ''he led the donkeys through the cave, down to the river, and then hid the gold down there somewhere?''

''Yeah, but remember the waybill. He hid the gold where a rock with the visage of a demon is looking at it.''

Her voice was weary with frustration. ''You don't think we have the wrong cave?''

''No, but we can look again tomorrow—just to be sure.''

She leaned back against the cave wall tiredly. ''Blessed St. Matthew, we're never going to find the gold.'' For the first time since I met the sister, I heard defeat in her voice.

Chapter Sixteen

Before sunrise next morning, we began scouring the east slope of the mountain. We looked under, around, and beside every juniper, mesquite, bull nettle, and patch of buffalo grass we could find.

By mid-morning, we had covered every inch.

No cave, except ours.

We plopped to the ground in the shade of a large juniper, none of us wanting to voice our disappointment. I opened the canteen and handed it to Alicia who sipped daintily and passed it on to Sister Rossetta.

Alicia tried to keep our spirits up. "Maybe we just overlooked it."

"No." Sister Rossetta shook her head, giving me a look of resignation. "I think Mr. Burnett is right. Father Kino hid the gold elsewhere."

"Well, I don't know about you two," Alicia chirped. "But I'm hungry. I say we whip up a batch of gravy and biscuits. Of course, the biscuits will have to be flat. We don't have any baking powder."

With a chuckle, I rose, helped them to their feet, and we headed across the slope to the cave entrance. "I'll get a fire going. While you ladies do the honors, I'll go check on the horses."

As I trekked over the hilltop and down to the tree covered riverbank below, I studied our problem with the gold. First, we had to find the original cave opening at the river. It had to be back south of the boulders. If it had opened below the sheer limestone bluff, the cave-in would have crushed it. We would have found boulders at the end instead of a sandy bed.

I glanced over my left shoulder at the boulders some half mile behind me. No question in my mind. The cave was somewhere south of the slope.

I hesitated after removing the limbs from the mouth of the sinkhole where I had corralled the ponies. The pool of sweet water had grown larger, taking in almost a third of the sandy bed. When I headed for the horses, my feet sunk in the sand, which was the consistency of black strap syrup. When I was leading the horses out of the sinkhole, my chestnut's hind leg sunk in the sand, but he pulled it out easily. I was too busy with other things on my mind to wonder about the sand. Later, I would remember, and regret.

"How can you be sure?" Alicia arched an eyebrow. "The cave might have cut across far enough back in the mountain that the landslide didn't affect it."

I couldn't argue with her. We had twisted and turned so many times in that cave that I couldn't hazard a guess where we were. "So how do we figure out where to start looking for the cave opening?"

Sister Rossetta looked from Alicia to me. "Why, we go back through the cave and make a map. Then we come back outside and trace the map across the hill. Simple."

"Huh?" My jaw dropped open.

She pointed to the cave opening. "We know it starts off going north. We'll simply draw a map as we step it off. Surely, the three of us can figure out directions each time the shaft takes a different angle. At least, we can come close to the exit."

Alicia and I looked at each other and shrugged, neither enthusiastic over her suggestion. "But the bends and curves, Sister. That's the problem," I protested. "Down in the cave, it's hard to tell when you angle off."

A bright smile dimpled her cheeks. "What if one of us brings up the rear by about fifty or sixty feet. We remain in the middle of the tunnel. If it begins curving to the left, the leader's light will move closer to the wall."

My first impulse was to dismiss the suggestion as nothing more than a fanciful idea, but before I could say a word, Alicia broke in. "That just might work, Jack."

"Huh?"

"Yes. Think about it. We'll stop at the first bend. You and Sister Rossetta go ahead. I'll remain behind until the light disappears around a bend, and then I'll give you a shout. We can draw the map in pieces until we reach the bottom."

I started to argue. No way such a far-fetched idea would pay off, but I knew from the tip of my head to the bottom of my feet that the only way I'd have any peace about the matter was to follow their fancy.

"Well, then. Let's give it a shot."

We had no pencil or ink, so Alicia gathered several chunks of charcoal from the ashes of the campfire and tore a large square from a sheet of oilcloth.

"I'm all set," she said, oilcloth in one hand, a lantern in the other.

Sister Rossetta nodded. "Me too."

I gave a shake of my head. "Well, then ladies. Let's get it done."

Mapping the cave took twice as long as our first journey through the twisting tunnel. At each bend, Sister Rossetta and I waited for Alicia to catch up, spread the oilcloth on the floor, then freehand the route of the cave.

When we emerged from the cave much later, stars filled the sky. We were hot and sweaty and the cool breeze off the river below was a welcome relief.

"Before we eat," said Sister Rossetta, breaking the silence. "I think I'll go down to the river and freshen up. I have another habit. I can wash this one and it should dry by morning. I can't spend another night with all this dirt and grit on me."

"I'll go with you, Sister," said Alicia. "I'd like to clean up too."

I hesitated. Not being sure about the whereabouts of Red or his boys, I didn't want the ladies off by themselves. "Sorry, Sister, but I can't let you go. Those owlhoots might be out there watching."

Sister Rossetta turned her face to me. The starlight lit her smile with a bluish cast. "Then I suppose you'll just have to go down there with us, Mr. Burnett."

I stammered and stuttered. "But. . . ."

She rose and waved her hand at me as if to dismiss

any concerns. "Shush. We'll find some willows to go behind. You can stand on the sandbar watching for those miscreants if you want. Personally, I think they're back in Austin City." She paused. "No offense, but it wouldn't hurt you to wade out into the river yourself."

I glanced at Alicia who gave me a cryptic smile. Even in the starlight, I could see the laughter in her eyes and on her lips.

So we traipsed down the hill and for the next thirty minutes, did our best to remove some of the dirt and sweat. I even removed my boots, jammed my rifle butt in the sand and soaped up a good lather on me, clothes and all.

Back in the cave, we opted for a cold supper of tortillas and jerky, washed down with sweet water. When I was a youngster, I was told that most of us drop off to sleep in less than seven minutes. I don't know if that's generally true or not, but that night, I wasn't awake at the end of the first minute.

Next morning, our menu for breakfast was the same we had for supper—tortillas and jerky—except this time we heated the tortillas and brewed a pot of coffee. After breakfast, we spread the map, aligning it with the cave, ready to trace the route of the cave across the top of the mountain.

"Ready, ladies?" I threw a shovel and grubbing hoe over my shoulder.

"Lead out, Mr. Burnett."

In addition to the directions, Alicia had jotted down the number of steps she had taken from one point to the next. We wandered up and down and over and around that hill. The map finally led across the slope of boulders, a difficult expanse for us to cross, but we managed.

Finally, we reached the end of the map. We looked around. We stood at the base of the hill on the north side of the slope.

"Is this it, do you think?" Alicia nodded to the rocky ground covered with patches of wild grass growing from the pockets of soil.

I looked around. Up river, all I saw was the green water flowing toward us, then curving around the sandbar on which we stood. To the west was Black Mountain, the mouth of the pass filled with boulders. Back south, the river looked no different that it did on the north side.

"Probably close enough."

Sister Rossetta peered along the east bank of the river. "Do you see anything like the boulder Father Kino described?"

I had already given the east riverbank a cursory glance. It didn't take more than that to see that there were no boulders along the shoreline. As much as I hated to disappoint the sister, we had run up against the wall, and the only way we could turn now was back.

I let my gaze wander idly over the river and surrounding hills. Despite the fact I had never truly expected any gold, I had not be able to shake a single, tiny, immutable hope deep inside that kept believing, until now. Now the hope vanished.

Despite my disappointment, I was impressed with the beauty of the river and the green hills. The riverbank near where I had corralled our ponies was lush with vegetation. Upstream, the river cut west, disappearing behind Black Mountain.

The source of the name Black Mountain was obvious, for the rock and soil were much darker than the surrounding hills of white limestone. I wondered who owned the land. Anyone? Probably. But a jasper could do a lot worse than settling in country like this. One fact was certain: There was plenty of water for a man's herd.

The shoreline along the mountain was the same as on my side of the river. I watched the cool water sweep under the overhanging willow limbs, and if I listened hard, I could hear the swish of the water brushing against the leaves.

Suddenly, I froze.

Two hundred yards across the river, a large stone with angular features protruded from a stand of riverbank willows. I studied the gray rock.

Twenty feet from top to bottom and eight to ten in width, it appeared to be a massive shard of rock that had split from an overhanging ledge forty feet above. The face of the ledge was worn smooth, mute testimony that the fracture had occurred in millenniums past.

The impact of the slab when it struck ground split the top, leaving two upthrusts, which to a man like Father Kino could have appeared as horns. The weather had worn off the softer limestone, leaving a knot the size of a washtub in the middle of the slab just where a nose might be.

I blinked once or twice, then just in case I was imagining things, moved a few steps to my left for a different perspective.

Alicia stopped at my shoulder. "What are you looking at, Jack?"

I nodded at the stone. "Over there. Across the river. See that large gray rock?"

Sister Rossetta jumped up and clapped her hands together. "That's it. That's the boulder Father Kino wrote about. It must be."

"Whoa, Sister," I said, chuckling. "Don't go getting your hopes up again."

"But Jack," said Alicia, laying her hand on my arm. "It could be." She stepped back and looked at the ground at our feet. "If Father Kino came out somewhere around here, he could have spotted the cave across the river."

I didn't want to discourage them, but at the same time, there was no sense in being disappointed again. "How do you know there's a cave there. Look. The willows hide everything."

"Let's go see," said Sister Rossetta, wading into the river.

I laughed and grabbed her arm, pulling her back. "Hold on, Sister, hold on. If anybody goes, it'll be me. You and Miss Alicia wait right here. I'll get my pony and swim him across. If there's a cave, we'll move our camp back across the river."

She pushed me toward the hobbled animals. "All right then, hurry."

Alicia laughed, and I joined in. Right then, I think I would have gladly cut off an arm to make them happy.

I rode the chestnut bareback into the river upstream of the slab. The current caught us and pushed us downriver. We reached shore only a couple yards below the slab. I waded ashore and tied the chestnut to a willow. I peered up at the slab towering over me. There was nothing to suggest eyes, so I looked in the general direction the washtub-sized nose was pointing.

My heart skipped a beat. Behind a thick tangle of willows and briars almost fifty feet in breadth, I spotted what appeared to be a dark opening in the side of the mountain. I cocked my head for a better look, thinking that I was simply staring at a shadow.

It was a cave. For a moment, time seemed to freeze. My ears pounded. Could the waybill be true?

Looking around, I found a broken branch that had been washed ashore. I used it to poke through the underbrush ahead of me just in case some snakes had decided they wanted to rest in a cool spot. Slowly, I elbowed into the tangle.

Shouts drifted across the river. I looked back. Alicia and Sister Rossetta stood in the water at the edge of the sandbar. I waved and motioned for them to just hold their britches.

The briars scraped my skin, deep enough in places that a thin line of pink appeared against my dark skin. Blackberry briars and honeysuckle vines wove a thick snarl over the small willows, forcing me to skirt the knot. I ducked to peer through a small opening in the tangle for a better look at the cave.

My hopes crashed.

The cave was filled with a jumble of rocks.

Muttering a curse, I shouldered on through the remainder of the briars, ignoring the thorns and snags, stopping in the mouth. Frustrated, I stared at the cave. It was only four or five feet high—too low for loaded burros.

Then, a thought hit me. Too low for burros, but not

too low for a man. I squatted in the mouth and studied the roof of the cave. From what little I could see, the roof had not caved in.

What if . . .

Behind me, Alicia and Sister Rossetta were shouting. I ignored them, instead grabbing the rocks and pulling them from the mouth of the cave. My forearm ached, but it had just about healed, so I didn't mind working it more than usual.

I pulled the rocks from the top of the jumble, revealing a few more feet of the roof. My pulse raced. There was no sign of a cave-in. I allowed myself to complete the question that had popped into my mind. What if Father Kino had unloaded the burros here, cached the gold in this cave, and filled in the mouth with rocks?

Excited, I backed out of the cave and waved to Alicia and Sister Rossetta. I knew if I didn't bring them over, they'd end up swimming.

An hour later, we were back at the cave, staring at the rocks filling it. "Take a look," I said, indicating the roof of the cave. "If this had been a cave-in, the ceiling would have fallen. It hasn't. It looks to me that someone jammed the cave with rocks to make anyone passing think it had caved in."

We started pulling rocks out. I tugged them from the jumble and rolled them back to Alicia who, with Sister Rossetta's help, shoved them from the cave opening. The task went slowly, but gradually we worked our way deeper into the cave.

By sunset, we had worked our way ten feet deep into the narrow cave. I paused while rolling out a large boulder. I was hot and sweaty, dirty and hungry. "It's time for us to get back across the river. I'll picket the horses near the cave so we can get an early start.''

Sister Rossetta looked past me at the wall of rocks. ''You think it's much farther, Mr. Burnett?''

''Beats me, Sister.'' I shrugged. ''Come tomorrow morning, we'll start pulling them out again.''

Chapter Seventeen

I was tired.

How tired, I didn't realize until the next morning, when I awakened in the cave with a half-eaten tortilla in one hand and an untouched slab of jerky in my other. Sister Rossetta was leaning against the cave wall, her chin on her chest, and Alicia was curled in a ball on the floor.

I awakened them, and slowly we managed to scrub the sleep from our eyes and shake the weariness from our bones. Despite the anticipation of the gold awaiting us, our sore muscles groaned with each movement. While I bridled and fed our ponies, the ladies whipped up some grub. Thirty minutes later, we swam the river and pulled up at the cave.

I crawled back inside and began shoving boulders out to Alicia who in turned rolled them to Sister Rossetta. Within a few minutes, I noticed, to my surprise, the roof of the cave began ascending. I pulled out a rock about half the size of my saddle, and there was nothing behind it, just darkness. A musty smell rolled out.

We were through.

"Here it is!" I shouted. "The rocks end here. It looks like a room or some kind of chamber on the other side."

Abruptly, a spade-headed rattlesnake filled the opening.

"*Yaaaah!*" I screamed, leaping back and bumping into Alicia who fell back into Sister Rossetta. "Out! out!" I shouted, pushing them ahead of me.

I sent Alicia and Sister Rossetta down to the river's edge while I remained to the side of the mouth, anxious to see just where that rattler went. I gripped the pole I had first used to probe the underbrush. If he came toward me, he was dead.

He paused in the mouth of the cave, just before reaching the scythe of sunlight cast on the floor of the cave. I've seen larger rattlesnakes, but the truth is, any rattler is a large one to me. He was between four and five feet long, and I reckon he thought he owned the world for he slithered out of that cave and turned straight toward me.

I jabbed the end of the pole at his head, intending on smashing that ugly skull on the rocks below. I would have smashed it too, but I missed the head. I backed up and jabbed again, and again missed. Four more times I backed up and jabbed before finally hitting him.

His head crunched, and instinctively, his tail whipped forward and curled around the pole. His rattles whined. I put my weight on the pole and tried my best to twist and grind it through his head.

Suddenly, I stepped back and yanked the pole free. The rattler lay writhing and thrashing on the rocks.

"He's dead," I said, glancing at the women. But, to be on the safe side, I slipped the tip of the pole under him and flipped him several feet through the air into the river downstream of Sister Rossetta and Alicia.

He hit with a splash and sank.

I looked back around, just in time to see Sister Rossetta head for the cave. "Stop!" I shouted. "Don't go back in there."

She frowned at me, then realization erased the frown. "You mean . . ."

"Yeah. Where's there's one, there's bound to be more."

I crossed the river and returned with the coal oil lanterns. After easing just inside the cave and using the pole to dislodge a few more rocks to enlarge the opening to the inner chamber, we gathered dry brush, and I tossed it into the breach, each time expecting more rattlers to come pouring out. To our surprise and relief, none did. Maybe there were no more.

Suddenly, I heard that familiar, terrifying hum that caused my heart to leap up in my throat. I swallowed hard. There were more inside.

Gingerly, I continued tossing branches through the gap. When I figured we had enough brush inside, I removed the globe, unscrewed the fuel cap on one of the lanterns, lit the wick and turned the flame high. I looked back at Alicia and Sister Rossetta. "Okay, get clear. When I toss this in, any rattlers inside are coming out, and they'll be mighty unfriendly if anyone should try to stop them."

Taking a deep breath, I lobbed the lantern through the opening into the inner chamber. Moments later, there came a whoosh, and a bright burst of fire lit the opening.

I scrabbled out to join Alicia and Sister Rossetta. We all perched on boulders, well out of the reach of any rattlesnakes.

Within moments, a dark, acrid smoke billowed from the cave.

Alicia gasped and pointed. "Look! Look at the snakes!"

We had hit a nest. I counted over twenty rattlesnakes, of various sizes, scooting out of the cave, fleeing the fire and smoke. With each one that emerged and disappeared into the underbrush, my desire for the gold grew less and less.

The heat was so intense, it burned the tangle of briars for twenty feet around the mouth of the cave. If we were lucky, maybe we had driven the rattlers all away.

I crossed my fingers. I sure wasn't anxious to go back inside and start poking around again. But I did, after the fire had burned out a couple hours later.

We saw no more snakes, but I didn't kid myself. The ones the fire had not incinerated, the heat had driven them up into the fissures in the mountain from which they came. I glanced at the ledge above us. I'd be willing to give goods a bunch of them were up there now, watching us with murder in their hearts.

And I didn't keep my musings to myself.

Alicia looked fearfully at the ledge above. "What if they come over the edge?"

"They won't." I shook my head. "They're like any living creature. They won't go in harm's way."

She looked at me hopefully. "Really?"

With a nonchalance I didn't feel, I replied, "Yeah, so don't worry."

Without warning, a dark object flashed by our eyes and slammed to the ground in front of us. I looked down into the eyes of an infuriated rattlesnake.

Needless to say, the three of us scattered like a covey of quail, gathering down at the river's edge. Sister Rossetta was as pale as her bonnet. Alicia, fair-complexioned anyway, was as white as the feathers on a duck's back. I didn't figure I looked any better.

"Now what?" Sister Rossetta looked up at me.

We were standing knee deep in the swirling water, our eyes fixed on the cave and the ledge above. "Can't rightly say, Sister."

Mother Nature answered the question for us.

We had been too absorbed in the cave and snakes to notice the dark clouds rolling in, but a peal of lightning and a rumble of thunder got our attention. Back south, above the hills, a gray veil of rain raced toward us.

I shook my head in wonder. Today had been one heck of a day. Chasing snakes, dodging snakes, wading in the river, and now caught out in the open with a rip-snorting storm approaching. Anyway you looked at it, we going to get wet and uncomfortable.

"Let's go, ladies," I said, heading for the ponies. "Let's get back to our cave."

The rain hit us in mid-river. Overhead, lightning crackled and snapped, filling the air with the smell of ozone.

Like blind men, we stumbled up the hill only to find our cave was a natural watercourse for runoff from the top of the hill. I tied the horses to a large juniper while the ladies began dragging our sodden gear from the cave.

The rain continued—a steady, blistering downpour without end. Finally, wet, muddy, disgusted, tired, and in general fed up with our plight, we had managed to string a tarp above us, laid a small fire that struggled against the gusting wind, and had coffee on the fire. I rigged up canvas walls of sorts, and using the shovel, scraped out a shallow ditch to carry the water around our camp. Night came early, and it was going to be a miserable one, but at least we'd have some coffee and occasional heat from the fire.

We couldn't get comfortable, so we worked on our shelter, stretching, staking, and fastening the bottom of the canvas walls to the ground. By midnight, we were actually drying off.

Alicia laughed. "Who knows? We might even get dry enough to sleep."

A crack of lightning was her answer.

The fire was hot, but we never dried out, although we did sleep in bits and pieces between thundering bolts lancing the countryside. I glanced at Sister Rossetta, who was running her fingers over her beads, silently forming her prayers.

Several times, I wished we had made camp lower on the hill, but now all we could do was sit tight and hope the sister's prayers worked.

We had our share of lightning strikes, but for some reason Black Mountain attracted most of the bolts. They cracked and popped at the mountain. The air tingled with static electricity, and more than once, I felt like we were nothing more than a lightning rod at which the thunderbolts were taking aim. At times across the river, the lightning appeared to be dancing across the rocky crest of Black Mountain like a troop of those high society ballerinas I read about in the newspaper in Fort Worth.

Sometime during the early morning, I slept, but sharp cracks and drawn-out rumbling continued to awaken me. I looked around. Alicia slept with her head on a saddle and Sister Rossetta slumbered on a tarp spread in one corner. I heard a strange roaring, one I had not heard before. I peered into the darkness, into the sheeting rain. The raging lightning cracked, illumining the river with a ghostly glow, which vanished almost immediately. I squinted into the storm, but all I could make out were the vague outlines of the mountains across the river. Had the storm dislodged a boulder and sent it tumbling down to the river?

The roaring continued.

Slowly, the darkness faded into a dismal gray morning. By now the lightning had passed, but the rain continued unabated. Outside our shelter, water coursed downhill in torrents toward the river. I heard someone behind me stir. I looked around as Alicia sat up and stretched her arms.

"Ohhh, I'm stiff."

I chuckled. "Coffee's hot. That'll help." I turned back to the steady rain.

She poured some and joined me. "At least the lightning has stopped."

Sister Rossetta came to stand by us. "Can you see anything?"

"No, still too dark."

She stuck her hands, palms up, into the rain and

washed her face. "What's that sound? A roar. I didn't hear it last night."

"I don't know. With all this wind and rain, it's hard to pinpoint a direction."

But when the sun rose and the shadows disappeared on the river, we saw the source of the roaring.

Sister Rossetta exclaimed, "Dear St. Matthew!"

Alicia gasped, and I cursed.

Black Mountain had split from the rim to the cave below, spilling rocks and boulders to either side of what had once been the mouth of the cave, forming a three-sided chimney. A torrent of water was spewing from the base of the chimney like water out a faucet.

The blackened underbrush between the cave and the river's edge was covered with layers of sand and rock disgorged from the cave.

Numbed, I plopped to the ground, ignoring the mud.

By mid-morning, the rain ceased. We sat on the hill staring down at the cave. The torrent had lessened considerably, but water still gushed from the cave down to the river.

I felt Sister Rossetta's eyes on me. I knew exactly what she was thinking, because I had the same, far-fetched idea. "I'll get the horses. We need to get over there fast." I nodded upriver. "I wouldn't be surprised to see the river start rising in a couple hours." Quickly I saddled the horses and fastened the saddlebags snugly behind the cantle. I figured with the heavy current, we might need more than just a handful of mane to stick to our pony's back.

I snapped the other horses to a loose rein and quickly lashed our gear to them despite Sister Rossetta's protest I was taking too much time.

"Sister," I explained in exasperation, "once we get over there, we're not coming back. We won't be able to get back."

The river was muddy and swift. It had already risen almost a foot. We entered a couple hundred yards above the cave, coming ashore a few yards below the fan-shaped spread of sand that had washed from the shattered cave. To the right of the cave, a narrow trail led to the top. We tied the ponies at the base of the trail and gingerly made our way over the layers of newly deposited sand to the cave that had now been split open like a hog at the winter butchering.

A stream of water still ran from where the mouth had been, cutting a narrow groove in the wet sand. Some of the rocks that had once blocked the cave had washed away, but a few remained, marking the location of the wall. Beyond the rocks was a sandy bed almost twenty feet square. If there had been gold behind the rocks, that's where it would have been. Was it there now, just below the sand?

A light drizzle began.

I peered up the chimney, its black walls towering to the gray sky. I dropped my gaze back to the sandy area before me.

I handed Alicia the hoe. I took the shovel and perched on the wall of rocks. "You both wait here. I want to see how deep this sand is." With a grunt, I kicked the blade deep in the sand. Favoring my healing forearm, I tossed the first load aside and returned to the hole.

Sister Rossetta gasped.

"Look!" shouted Alicia.

I didn't have to look, for in the bottom of the hole,

blood squirted from the writhing body of a rattlesnake I'd sliced in half. I jumped back, then leaped forward, slamming the tip of the blade down on the twisting snake again.

I looked around at Alicia and Sister Rossetta in disbelief. "Now we've got snakes buried in the sand."

They were too busy looking at the sand at their feet to answer.

I scooped up the snake and tossed it aside, then handed Alicia the shovel. "Let me have the grubbing hoe. If I pull up another rattler, I want to be a few feet from him."

The drizzle grew heavier.

Hefting the heavy hoe over my head awkwardly, I dug into the sand and jerked up a chunk of wet soil. If this was the right cave, here is where the gold had to be. It was too heavy to be washed out by the flood of water, despite its force.

I stepped forward and swung the grubbing hoe. It sunk to the handle in the wet sand. I yanked out a clod of sand, and swung again, digging down through the sand.

Suddenly, the blade of the grubbing hoe bounced off an object, the vibration stinging my hands, burning the almost healed crack in my forearm. "Must have hit rock," I muttered, swinging again.

The blade stuck. Cursing under my breath, I yanked, and a dark, square shape about the size of a can of peaches came flying out, striking the ground beside me with a thud. I dodged.

Digging up the rattlesnake had shaken me. As spooked as I was, I would have jumped at anything.

"What is it?" Sister Rossetta cocked her head. "A rock?"

I glanced at it. Just as I started to agree with her, I noticed that the surface the rock appeared to be peeling. I touched the corner of the hoe blade to curling skin and tugged.

A square of canvas fell off, revealing a dull yellow flash of gold.

Chapter Eighteen

I dropped the hoe and grabbed the gold. With trembling fingers, I peeled the rotten canvas away. Alicia and Sister Rossetta gasped in awe. The bar was about half the size of an adobe brick, roughly rectangular and weighing about twenty pounds.

With rain running down our faces, we grinned like possums with full bellies. "Here you are, Sister. Your school and hospital."

I returned to my digging, working at the twenty-foot-square area methodically, left to right, a foot at a time.

I chopped down with the hoe. Nothing on the first sweep across. On the second sweep, I pulled out another bar. On the next chop, I pulled out half of another rattlesnake that sent us dancing back toward the river.

The excitement over the discovery of the gold and the unexpected encounters with the rattlesnakes had drained the blood from Sister Rossetta and Alicia's faces. I didn't figure there was much color in mine either.

I peered into the trenches I'd dug. Three feet wide, twenty feet long. No more gold. No more rattlesnakes. The gold must be farther out. I hesitated, noticing the water gathering in the bottom of the trench. I figured it was just the rain. If I had known better, I would have worked faster.

Taking a deep breath, I stepped into the water. I felt solid rock beneath my feet. Then I stepped out onto the sand. My feet sunk to my ankles, but I slogged to the middle of the area and began digging again. On my first swing, I hit a solid object. I yanked. Another bar of gold popped out. It hit the ground behind me and rolled into the trench.

I grinned at Alicia. "Here it is. I've found it." I pulled my feet out of the sucking sand.

Both Sister Rossetta and Alicia hurried forward into the trench, sloshing through the rising water. Sister Rossetta stacked the bar with the other one.

The next three times I chopped into the sand, I pulled out another bar, but each time I sunk in almost to the top of my boots.

Suddenly, on the far side of the sandy bed, a pool of water appeared along the base of the chimney. And then I remembered the sinkhole where I had corralled the horses.

A cold dread raced through my body.

I looked around at the river. It had risen noticeably in the thirty minutes we had been here. I turned back to the gold and dug frantically. "Hurry!" I shouted. "Get as much as we can."

The water at the base of the chimney crept toward me. I knew exactly what was going to happen, the same thing that had taken place back at the corral. The water from the rising river was permeating the sand, turning it to quicksand. Within minutes, the gold would sink.

"What's wrong?" Sister Rossetta looked at me and then picked up another bar.

"I'll explain later, Sister. Right now we got to work fast."

In the next few minutes, I didn't count the number of bars we pulled out. I was too busy watching the water creeping toward us. Before I knew it, the water had covered the entire bed, and the rain was falling harder.

The blade of the hoe caught another object, this one much heavier. I strained to heave it from the sucking sand. Suddenly, I started sinking.

With a shout, I fell backward. In the next instant, Alicia and Sister Rossetta were at my side, lifting me to my feet. I held onto the handle with my left hand and backed to the rock. They both grabbed the handle and began tugging with me.

Moments later, the corner of a wooden rack emerged from the sand. I couldn't believe our luck.

We had latched onto an entire packsaddle with its gold still lashed to it.

Clenching my teeth against the pain in my forearm, I grunted and hauled back.

With the three of us, the rack eased forward. Only a few feet to the rock ledge on which we stood, but the sand was growing more saturated with water.

The weight of the gold increased.

The rain grew heavier.

We grunted; we groaned.

Without warning, we lurched back, breaking away

from the rack. We fell on the wet sand. I still held the hoe handle, but the blade was missing. The weight of the gold had ripped the blade from the handle.

Alicia jumped to her feet and waded into the sand after the gold. Almost instantly, she sank up to her waist. She screamed and turned back to us. I reached out with both hands and grabbed her arm.

I couldn't budge her. The suction holding her was powerful. "Lay toward us," I told her in a calm, firm voice.

Her eyes widened with alarm. She hesitated.

I held her hands tightly. "Do what I say, Alicia. I'll take care of you. Now lay on the sand toward me."

With a trusting smile, she did as I said.

Leaning forward broke the vacuum holding her in the quicksand, and by distributing her body weight over the sand, we managed to slide her onto the rock ledge on which we stood.

I helped Alicia to her feet and held her tightly. We were all shaken.

She shook her head. "I just wanted to get the gold."

The water began pooling over the top of the quicksand. "It's gone now."

Sister Rossetta sighed. "What happened? Why did it sink?"

I gestured to the mountains around us. "They're shot through with fissures and chimneys. This one," I explained, nodding to the bed at our feet, "this one must be connected to the river somehow. Maybe it was the rising water. Who knows?"

"Then why hasn't it happened before. The gold was there. Surely the river has flooded since Father Kino hid the gold."

We continued staring at the quicksand, imagining

the wealth of gold sinking deeper and deeper. The rain beat against us, but we ignored it. ''Beats me, Sister. Maybe the mountain splitting apart had something to do with it. I don't know.''

''At least,'' Alicia said, ''we have some of the gold.''

We had pulled out twenty-eight bars.

''Well over a hundred thousand dollars, Sister. More than enough for your hospital and school.''

Despite the sand and water on her face, her smile was dazzling. She turned her eyes to the heavens. ''Thank you, Holy Father St. Matthew.''

I packed the bars in our saddlebags. At twenty pounds each, eight or ten bars added considerable weight for our ponies to carry.

The river continued rising. By the time we were packed and heading up the narrow trail to the top of Black Mountain, the flood waters were within a couple feet of the quicksand.

Just before sundown, the rain stopped. The trace to Oak Hill was two feet deep in sticky mud, slowing our progress. We decided on a cold camp that night. No fire to give our location away.

Next morning, we built a small fire for coffee, then pushed out, reaching Oak Hill just before noon. We rode straight through the small village, ignoring the curious looks cast our way. Outside of Oak Hill, the muddy trace hit limestone, and we picked up the pace.

''Not long now, ladies,'' I announced. ''Another ten or twelve miles.''

We rode in silence. The miles fell behind.

Finally, we topped the last hill overlooking Austin

City. The rising waters of the muddy Colorado were just below us. Swirling and churning, they pushed south to the ferry some four miles distant. I glanced at Alicia. Her hair hung in dirty strings, her clothes were grimy and torn, but when she looked at me, all I saw were the smile on her lips and the laughter in her eyes. "Anything wrong?"

"Huh? Oh no." I turned back to the road. My ears burned.

Maybe she read my mind, for she asked, "What are your plans now, Jack?"

I held my arm up, displaying my stained and tattered shirt sleeve. I chuckled. "Get a hot bath and clean clothes."

They both laughed. "Why don't you go back to the coast with us, Mr. Burnett?" Sister Rossetta eyed me seriously. "We're going to need help building the hospital and school."

"You're going back to the coast too, huh?" I directed the question to Alicia.

"Might as well. My aunt made it plain she doesn't want me or the girls here. Besides, after all I've gone through for the gold, I think I'd like to see some good come from it."

We headed along the river road toward the ferry that would transport us across the Colorado River. Now that our journey was growing to a close, I felt a sense of emptiness.

Ahead, the narrow road curved through a thick stand of juniper. Just as we entered the patch, my chestnut stumbled and crashed to his knees, sending me sprawling.

"What the . . ." I yelled, scrambling to my feet, ready to give that piece of crowbait a good kick. The chestnut hobbled to his feet, favoring his front left. I winced as I knelt and felt his knee and pastern. There was some sponginess, but I couldn't feel a break. I sighed with relief. I didn't want to have to shoot the animal. He'd been a good pony.

"You all right, Jack?"

I glanced at Alicia. "Yeah."

"What about the horse?"

"He's alright. Can't ride him anymore, though." Quickly, I removed the saddlebags and laid them in at the side of the trail after which I yanked the saddle from the chestnut's back and dropped it on top of the saddlebags, which was a piece of pure dumb luck.

Suddenly, a child's scream echoed down the trail followed by the clattering of hooves against the limestone trail. I looked up just as Red and Greasy Hair rode up, six-guns drawn and leveled at us. Red gave us a plug-ugly sneer and drawled, "Just you folks stay nice and calm, you hear? And you, cowboy, you keep them hands where I can see 'em."

Greasy Hair rode up to Alicia and opened the bulging saddlebags. His eyes grew wide when he saw the contents. "Bejeebees, Red. They done found the gold. You believe it? They done gone and found the gold."

Red's expression didn't change. He kept his eyes narrowed on me.

I laid my hands on the chestnut's back, trying to come up with some kind of plan. I figured I could spook the animal which might give me a second or two. Maybe that would be enough time. I glanced sidelong at Greasy Hair.

"Don't try nothing, cowboy," he said, his tone warning. "I don't expect you'd mind risking a slug, but there's two little girls up the road there that you better think about.''

Sister Rossetta and Alicia gasped.

Red sneered. ''Yep. You guessed right. We rode into Austin and picked up two little girls you folks happen to know.''

He gave a whistle, and moments later, the third owlhoot came riding around the bend leading a pony on which Carmaline and Mary Elizabeth rode. They began crying when they recognized Alicia and Sister Rossetta.

I knew then I'd do whatever Red wanted.

A sneer twisted Red's lips. ''A swap, cowboy. Two girls for the gold.''

Sister Rossetta and Alicia hurried to the girls. I stepped back and held my hands over my head. ''It's yours.'' I glanced at my saddle on the ground. It lay on top of my saddlebags. Only a couple strings showed. I hoped the outlaw would think they were part of the saddle.

He gave an ugly laugh. ''Yeah, I know.'' He nodded to our ponies. ''Hand me them reins.''

I did as he ordered.

''Reckon you can walk on in,'' he said, sneering. ''See how you like it.''

Off to my right, Alicia and Sister Rossetta were hugging the girls, murmuring soothing words. The older jasper grinned wickedly.

''You know, I'll come after you.'' I stared coldly at the sneering outlaw.

''So what? By the time you get to Austin City, we'll be long gone.'' He hesitated, noting my saddle on the ground. ''Where's your saddlebag?''

I hooked my thumb at the saddle. "Don't have one. Right there is all I got."

He eyed me suspiciously. I tried to appear straightforward and open, hoping he wouldn't demand I turn the saddle over. Before he had a chance to reply, I added, "You could at least leave one horse for the nun and the girls."

His sneer broadened, and he forgot about my saddle. "Not a chance. Like I said, we'll be long gone. I ain't never kilt nobody except Comancheros, so I don't aim to start now. Just you don't give me no cause."

Sister Rossetta and Alicia had brought the girls back to my side. I stepped forward, placing myself between the ladies and Red. "You got what you want. Just leave us be."

He grinned a twisted, crooked fissure on his bearded face. "So long, cowboy." He wheeled and started down the road while we stared after him. Greasy Hair and the old man fell in beside Red.

Sister Rossetta sighed. "At least we're safe, even if we don't have the gold."

I didn't have time to carry on a polite conversation. I kicked my saddle over and grabbed my saddle gun. "You still have this gold, Sister." I nodded to the saddlebags.

Her eyes grew wide. "It was under the saddle," I explained. "But I want the rest of it."

The relief in their eyes turned to alarm. "What do you mean, Jack?" Alicia stepped forward.

I headed to the river. All of us had worked too hard, too long, and faced too many dangers just to give up the gold. I was mad, and I planned on doing something about it. If I failed, at least I tried. "I'm going to get the rest of your gold back."

Alicia shook her head and grabbed my arms. "No, Jack. It's too dangerous. They'll kill you."

For a moment, I hesitated. I looked straight into her eyes. "Not me. I'm coming back."

She blinked against the tears filling her eyes. "I'll be here."

Sliding down the bank, I plunged into the swirling, churning waters, fighting my way into the current where I latched onto one of the numerous logs bobbing with the current.

My plan was hasty and filled with maybes, but it was the only idea I could come up with. The ferry was beyond a bend in the river. I figured if I could cut across the flooding river, I might intersect the ferry before it reached shore.

Muddy water splashed in my face, choking me. I clung desperately to the log, kicking my feet in an effort to make it move even faster. Ahead, the ferry left the west bank. My hopes soared. That meant it had to cross to the far bank, and then return to pick up Red and his cohorts.

A one way trip was thirty minutes. Now I had an hour.

I peered up at the west bank. Far ahead, Red and his partners loped along unconcerned, unaware I was following.

Smaller debris swept past me as I clung to the heavy log lumbering through the water. We seemed to be motionless, but the trees on the bank drifted behind us. I was moving, but not fast enough.

Several feet away, a square of lumber, like the tailgate of a wagon, drew even with me. On impulse, I released my grip on the log and swam for the board.

I dodged a couple logs, but as I skirted a third, the saddle gun caught on a limb and slipped from my hand. I lunged backward, clamping my legs together on the slim chance of snagging it.

I felt it slither through my knees, bounce off an ankle, and then it was gone.

Chapter Nineteen

With a curse, I turned back to the tailgate, but it had drifted several feet downstream. A tangle of underbrush swept over me, pushing me under the dark water.

I choked and clawed my way back to the surface. By now, the tailgate was almost twenty feet away. In burst of desperation, I swam after it despite the swirling floodwaters that grasped and tugged on my shirt and vest.

Finally, I caught up with the gate and pulled my weary body halfway up on it. My breath came in great gasps. Exhausted, I collapsed on the tailgate.

I lost track of time, but when I looked up, the exhaustion that had numbed my muscles vanished in an explosion of adrenaline. The ferry was within a hundred yards of the western shore.

And waiting impatiently for the lumbering raft was Red and his outlaw cohorts. I glanced over my shoulder.

Far upriver, four tiny dots stood on the riverbank—
too distant to discern features, but I knew who they
were.

Shifting my weight, I angled for the east bank, hoping to intercept the ferry on the return trip. Now I had
to worry about the owlhoots spotting me.

Behind me came more underbrush. I pulled some
of it to me, trying to break my outline, hoping those
jaspers would pay no attention to a snarl of brush in
the flooding river. The wrist-thick hemp rope stretching across the broad river floated just below the
surface.

I felt for my six-gun. It was still in the holster. I
shook my head in dismay. The Colt Navy was a ball
and cap. The grease had probably worked out of the
chamber and the powder was wet, which meant it
wouldn't fire. My only hope was that the percussion
caps would detonate, and maybe that explosion would
give me the time I needed. At that moment, I made a
solemn vow that the first thing I would do if I got out
of all this was plank down twenty-five greenbacks for
a metal cartridge Colt Peacemaker.

By now, the ferry had begun its return journey with
Red and his cohorts. Along the starboard side of the
ferry was a railing on the top of which were bolted a
series of iron doughnuts through which the rope extended before dropping back into the water.

The ferryboat captain stood in front of the rail, pulling on the rope, dragging the raft across the river.

Behind me and off to my right, an uprooted blackgum swept toward the ferry, half of its crown and root
system sticking out of the water.

Suddenly, I saw my chance.

The ferry's draw rope rode just below the surface,

and if the blackgum kept on course it would snag the rope. When it did, it would get the attention of those on the ferry, giving me the opportunity to climb aboard.

I hope.

Kicking hard, I drove my flimsy raft toward the east shore, hoping to be on the far side of the ferry when the blackgum hit the rope.

Shouts drifted across the turmoil of the river. I glanced over my shoulder as Red pointed out the tree and gestured frantically for Greasy Hair to help the ferryman pull the rope while the old outlaw tried to hold the horses. My eyes went to the saddlebags strung behind the saddle cantles. Our gold.

All four men were too busy looking behind them to spot me. I caught the front left corner of the ferry and climbed aboard, palming my old Navy Colt. To my relief, the chambers were still packed with grease. Maybe they would fire. Maybe not.

I don't know what the real explanation was, but it could be Mother Nature was tired of kicking me and the ladies around; could be our luck had changed; or could be for symmetry Holy St. Matthew decided to take a hand in the game.

Whatever the reason, just as I climbed on board, the blackgum struck the rope fifty feet behind the ferry, driving the rope down river and carrying the raft with it. The rope rose like some kind of sea monster from the muddy water and grew tight, so tight water popped from the vibrating strands of hemp.

The horses reared, yanking the old man's feet off the deck. "Down, blast you, git down," he shouted.

Red turned at the scream and spotted me. "Why

you . . .'' He grabbed for his six-gun, but I fired first. The cap exploded, but the six-gun didn't fire.

Red fired. A loud thrumming pop echoed his shot just as a powerful blow hit my waist just above my hip, knocking me back on my heels.

At that instant, the taut rope snapped.

The old ferryboat captain jumped overboard.

Greasy Hair leveled his six-gun at me, but just before he fired, the whistling rope whipped around and slapped him across his face, driving him back over the edge of the ferry into the swirling waters.

I dropped to my knees and fired again. This time, the powder exploded, and my slug knocked Red's leg from under him. He slammed to the deck. I rolled to my right, clicking another chamber in front of the hammer, at the same time, swinging the Navy Colt around on the old outlaw.

He had vanished along with the horses.

I jumped to my feet. Fifty feet down river, the horses swam frantically toward the bank. The old outlaw was nowhere to be seen.

Behind me, Red cursed. I spun as he fired from his prone position on the deck. His slug caught me in the shoulder, spinning me back around and sending me sprawling.

Digging my toes into the deck, I pivoted around on my belly and fired again.

Red lurched from the impact of the slug, jerking his head into his shoulder. He tried to raise his six-gun. Quickly, I thumbed the trigger back and squeezed off another shot, but the Colt misfired. I tried again. Another misfire.

Keeping his head against his shoulder, he glared at me with one eye, his teeth glistening like white fangs through his bushy red beard. The muzzle of his hand-gun wavered, dropped, then struggled to level on me.

I tried to roll aside, but my muscles refused to move. I forced my free hand to the six-gun, thumbing back the trigger and trying to line up my sights on Red.

Our teeth clenched, our muscles straining, we stared into each other's eyes, struggling for the strength to finish off the other. I squeezed the trigger slowly.

Suddenly, the Colt bucked in my hands, and the explosion deafened my ears.

The outlaw's head jerked back, the eyes wide with disbelief. And then they rolled up in the sockets, and his face slammed to the deck.

By now, the ferry was caught up in the flood, slowly revolving in the current. I struggled to my knees, clinging to the rope supports. The eastern bank swept past. I searched for the swimming horses, but they were nowhere in sight.

My shoulder throbbed, and the wound in my side burned like someone had stuck a branding iron to it. I struggled into a sitting position, leaning up against one of the rail posts. A wave of dizziness swept over me, and I squeezed my eyes closed in an effort to stop the spinning in my head.

Next thing I remembered was awakening in a bed in a small, whitewashed room with a cross on the wall.

Chapter Twenty

I could barely move. A thick layer of bandages was wrapped around my shoulder, waist, and forearm. On top of stopping a couple slugs, I had busted my forearm again.

Alicia sat on the edge of my bed, holding my hand while Sister Rossetta smiled knowingly at us. Both Carmaline and Mary Elizabeth sat at the foot of the bed. "The ferryboat captain got a rowboat and picked us up," Alicia explained.

Carmaline interrupted. "Yes, and then when we got to shore, we looked for you."

Sister Rossetta nodded. "Luckily, Mr. Burnett, the raft ran aground on the east bank. You were unconscious." She hesitated. "The other man, the one with the red hair, was dead."

I closed my eyes and slowly shook my head. "I didn't want to kill him, Sister, but I had no choice."

She nodded her understanding.

"What about the horses? Did you find the horses? The saddlebags were on them."

Alicia's fingers squeezed my hand. "The horses made it from the river, but the saddles and saddlebags were missing."

"They must have come off when the horses were swimming to shore."

I grimaced. "All that gold."

Sister Rossetta laid her hand on my arm. "Don't fret, Mr. Burnett. We still have the bag you saved. Eight bars."

Eight bars! I did some fast calculating. "Well, Sister. You still have about forty thousand. I reckon that should build you a nice school and hospital, huh?"

"Yes, Mr. Burnett, it most certainly will."

As soon as I got to my feet, I searched up and down the river on the remote chance the saddles might have washed ashore. I knew that they hadn't, that the gold had sunk straight down and was now probably buried in mud. But I had to try, if for no other reason than to be able to say I had made the effort.

A week later, we all sat at the sawbuck table in the mission dining room for the evening meal. After the blessing was said, Sister Rossetta passed me the platter of biscuits and said, "We leave for the coast in three days, Mr. Burnett. You need to make the arrangements for the five of us."

I paused in spooning redeye gravy over my biscuits. "Well now, hold on, Sister. I don't know that I have any plans of traipsing all that way back down to the coast."

She winked at Alicia. Carmaline and Mary Elizabeth giggled and ducked their heads. "Come now, Mr. Burnett," Sister Rossetta chided me. "I figure it's about time you and Alicia get married. How can you do it if you stay here?"

All I could do was gape at her while a hot blush rose up my neck and burned my ears. Was there anything that woman didn't have an opinion on? I looked at Alicia, and when I saw the smile on her lips I knew the answer.

"Well, Sister," I replied in my best Texas drawl. "I reckon someone has to go along with you ladies just to keep you out of trouble."

Alicia chuckled. "And you're the one?"

I fixed my eyes on hers. "Yes ma'am. I truly believe I am the one."

Her eyes danced. "So do I, Jack. So do I."